STARFISH COTTAGE

SHELL COVE BOOK 2

MEREDITH SUMMERS

CHAPTER ONE

"You only have two more days to come up with a plan to present at the town meeting."

Jules's words sent Maddie's anxiety levels skyrocketing, and she almost regretted answering the call. She loved talking to her cousin, but the clock was ticking, and she didn't need to be reminded.

Maddie set the phone on speaker and put it down on the kitchen counter so she could talk and continue working on refinishing the cabinets in the small beach cottage fixer-upper she'd just purchased.

"Don't worry. I have some good ideas brewing." Not really, but they would come. Wouldn't they?

"I hope so. We've only got one room request for next week."

Panic flared in Maddie's chest at her cousin's disappointed tone. Earlier in the summer, she and her two cousins, Jules and Gina, had inherited a motel on the coast of Maine from their grandmother. The Beachcomber Motel was in a gorgeous spot overlooking the ocean, and the town was quaint, but both were a bit run-down ever since the tourist traffic had dried up.

The motel and the town had potential. A popular televised baking contest that had chosen the town for one of their episodes had proven it was well worth reviving. Maddie was sure they could bring the town back to the way it had thrived in the past... *if* they could get the word out to ensure a steady stream of visitors.

All she had to do was think up another event that would have tourists flocking to their seaside town. It had seemed easy when she'd accepted the part-time job as head of the Shell Cove Chamber of Commerce. Now, not so much.

Maddie and her cousins had been lucky enough to get a loan for repairs on the Beachcomber and pay themselves a little salary for a while, but that would only last so long. She would have to come up with something really special—and quick—if she wanted to keep paying the mortgage for her little dream cottage.

"How many are still there?"

"Three, but two are leaving this week. Aggie seems like she's going to stay for a while, though," Jules said, laughing.

Feisty senior citizen Aggie Fletcher had been one of the contestants in the baking contest. She'd arrived too late for the contest, forcing Maddie's other cousin, Gina, to fill in. Aggie had eventually checked into the Beachcomber and had decided to stay for an extended vacation. Maddie wasn't sure if that extended stay had more to do with a certain elderly gentleman or the town itself. "I think maybe she's taken a liking to Henry."

"You noticed?"

"Who hasn't?" Maddie glanced out the kitchen window at the white sand beach and turquoise ocean, mesmerized by the view as her cousin filled her in on the goings-on at the motel. It had only been a few days since she'd last been there, but she still had her part in operating it and liked to stay informed. Since she'd been engrossed in the renovations at Starfish Cottage for the past few days, she hadn't had a recent update.

Glancing once at the electric sander, which she'd struggled with earlier, she picked up the piece of sandpaper that was supposed to fit on its belt. She wasn't good at gadgets and had failed at getting it to work. Oh well, nothing wrong with good old-fashioned elbow grease. She picked up a piece of sandpaper and got to work on the facing of the drawers beside the kitchen door.

The top one was smaller than the others and would be the perfect place to keep her day planner so that she could grab it quickly as she went out the door. Maddie was never without her day planner and didn't want it to get dusty or lost, especially since she'd be having someone come help her work on the cottage.

"Oh! And if you stop by, Gina made a rhubarb pie. You might want to avoid a sample though. I didn't tell her, but it's gross," Jules said.

Maddie smiled as she sanded the edges of the drawer. Gina was a novice pie baker and had taken to using the motel guests, and her cousins, as guinea pigs for her new concoctions.

"Thanks for the warning." Maddie put down the sandpaper and tugged at the drawer. The cabinets in the cottage must have been original. They were old wood with at least five coats of paint. All those coats of paint and the moisture of being near the ocean made the wood swell, and some of the drawers were stuck. Of course, the very one she wanted to use was the very one that wouldn't budge.

Maybe she would have to try harder. She grabbed the knob with both hands and tugged hard while exhaling loudly.

"What are you doing over there?" Jules asked.

"Trying to get a drawer open. I'm doing the refinishing myself. Can't afford to hire everything out." It had taken all her savings and the goodwill of the town banker, Henry, to help her buy the cottage.

"You hired Dex?" Jules sounded amused.

"No." Anyone but Dex. The carpenter they'd hired

to work on the Beachcomber was nice enough, but he was so disorganized that his methods just didn't jive with Maddie's style. She needed things to be neat and organized and planned out. "Rose's nephew, Frank, was available, so I hired him."

"Her nephew?" Jules sounded confused. "Rose is about eighty. Wouldn't her nephew be kind of old for carpentry work?"

"No. He's experienced. Not old."

"How come he wasn't around when we needed the work on the motel?"

"Frank is semiretired and only works a few months a year. Luckily, I got to snag him for the next two months."

"Didn't you like the job Dex did? I think he did a great job, and he did us some favors too."

He had done a good job and had very kindly offered to delay billing when he knew they didn't have the cash to pay. It wasn't that Maddie was unhappy with his work or with him. It was just that… hey, wait a minute. Why was Jules asking so many questions, and why did her voice have that weird tone to it? "Are you trying to fix me up with him?"

"No."

Jules's quick denial meant she definitely was.

"He has a girlfriend. Besides, I think Frank will be a better fit. Dex still has work to do at the Beachcomber." Hopefully just on the days when she wasn't there.

Just because Jules was happily dating Nick from the Shell Cove Bank didn't mean that Maddie was looking for anyone to date. She was too busy trying to renovate the cottage and think up an event to bring people to town.

Maddie gave another tug on the drawer. Still stuck. She planted her feet firmly in front, grabbed the small knob with both hands, and…

Ooompf!

The drawer suddenly decided to unstick. She fell backward, landing on the floor with a thud, the drawer still in her hand. A piece of paper floated out and landed beside her.

"Are you okay? What was that?" Jules's concern on the other end of the phone warmed her heart.

"I'm fine. I finally got that drawer opened."

Jules laughed. "Did you fall on your butt?"

"Yes." Maddie picked up the paper. It was a recipe. Etta Harper's Whisky Fudge. Etta Harper must have been the owner of the cottage. How interesting. Maddie remembered Pearl saying something about a mystery involved with the original owner. Did the recipe have something to do with it? And who ate whisky fudge?

A car pulled into the crushed-stone driveway. That must be Frank. Right on time. Maddie hung up, promising to stop by the Beachcomber later, dusted herself off, and went out front to meet Frank.

CHAPTER TWO

*M*addie's mood turned to disappointment when she saw a familiar pickup truck, dents and all, parked in front of the cottage. She frowned as Dex got out, his sun-kissed hair ruffling in the breeze as he chased a receipt that had spilled out of his truck when he got out.

"What are you doing here?" Oops. She hadn't meant to sound so confrontational.

"Well, good morning, Miss Sunshine." Dex shoved the receipt in his truck and turned his charming smile on her.

Maddie bristled at the annoying nickname he'd given her when he'd worked at the Beachcomber. So what if she was always optimistic? But she couldn't help but return the smile. Even though Dex could be annoyingly disorganized and maybe a little silly, he was still a nice guy.

"Morning." Maddie glanced into the truck. Maybe Frank was in the passenger seat. Had he brought Dex to assist him? If so, she hoped it wasn't for the entire project.

Dex squinted, shading his green eyes from the sun, and his gaze drifted to the ocean. Overhead, the caw of gulls mixed with the rhythmic sound of waves on the beach, just steps away. He took a deep breath, and Maddie couldn't help but do the same, tasting the sea air.

"Nice place you have here. Gram mentioned you bought this old cottage."

Maddie had developed somewhat of a close relationship with Dex's grandmother, Rose, who, along with her friends Leena and Pearl, had been the first to welcome her to Shell Cove. It was Rose that had suggested she take the Chamber of Commerce position. Which reminded her, she had better get back to work on her ideas for the presentation. She didn't have time to stand here chatting.

"Thanks. I love it here." She turned away from the ocean to see that Dex was now assessing the cottage, a slight frown creasing his brow. She could see why he was frowning. The place had been empty for years and was quite run-down. But she'd fallen in love with the little house with its large front porch and starfish-cutout shutters the moment she'd seen it. The location right on the beach was ideal. And even though it was small, it was the perfect size for her. She'd never imagined being able to afford beachfront property, but with the town being in bad shape, real estate prices were low.

"Needs a lot of work," he said.

"That's why I hired Frank."

"Yeah. He asked me to come… well, actually Rose did."

"To help him out?"

"No, actually he isn't feeling well, so Rose asked if I could do the job instead."

"Oh." Maddie tried not to sound disappointed. It wasn't that Dex didn't do a good job; it was just that she found his clutter and disorganized manner unsettling.

"Did you find a treasure in the house? There's rumors about it." Dex nodded toward her hand. She was still holding the recipe that had been in the drawer.

"Pearl said something about a mystery. I don't know if you'd call this a treasure, though. It's just a recipe." She held the brittle paper up. "Etta Harper's whisky fudge."

"Whisky fudge? Sounds good." Dex laughed. "I think Etta Harper was Deena's ancestor who started Saltwater Sweet Shop."

"No kidding. I bet Deena would like to have this then." Deena Walters' family had owned Saltwater Sweets, the candy store in town, for generations. People came for miles to buy their handmade chocolates and fudge. Maddie had indulged a few times herself, but she didn't remember seeing any whisky fudge. Maybe she could take a break while Dex set up for work and run the recipe over to Deena. His idea of setting up for work and hers were not the same thing, and watching the chaos would probably get on her nerves.

"So, Uncle Frank mentioned what you wanted to have done, but why don't you show me yourself?" Dex pulled a pencil from behind his ear and a thin piece of scrap wood out of his back pocket, presumably to use as a notepad.

Maddie shook her head and started toward the house. "Good idea. I'll get you situated, and then I have to run an errand."

DEX LOWERED THE TAILGATE OF HIS PICKUP TRUCK AND waved to Maddie as she drove off. She was as uptight as she'd been when he'd worked at the Beachcomber, but at least she hadn't made a fuss that he was here instead of Frank like his grandmother had warned she might.

Rose had told him to insist that Maddie take Dex as a replacement, which he'd thought was kind of strange. But Rose had simply said that Maddie was supposed to be working on bringing tourists to town, and she didn't want her to get distracted with Frank not being up to doing the job. The cottage was barely livable, and it needed work right away.

Dex could get on board with that. He knew Shell Cove needed tourist money to survive, and he loved the town. If Maddie needed to focus on that, he would do his best to make sure she didn't get distracted. The weird thing was he didn't think Uncle Frank was that sick. He'd seen him over at Ocean Brew sipping an iced coffee just that morning. Oh well. One never knew what Rose was up to. She was full of surprises, and that was one of the things he loved about her.

Dex had lived his whole life in Shell Cove, but he'd never been inside Starfish Cottage. It needed a lot of work but had potential. The bungalow had a small living room, dining area off to the side, and a kitchen with a window overlooking the ocean. Out back was a newer deck, which Maddie had already decorated with an inviting rattan sectional and pillows. The front had a porch that was missing more spindles than it had. The stairs opposite the front door led to two bedrooms and a shared bathroom on the second floor.

The flooring was scarred, the ceiling stained, and the plaster walls had holes, but it was perfect for one person. As he walked around looking for any structural damage that would need to be addressed first, he couldn't help but think about what he would do to improve the property if it were his. Extend the porch to wrap around, get rid of the dining area, and make the kitchen bigger. Install French doors to show off more of the exquisite ocean view. Maybe make the window over the sink bigger. They hadn't made the windows big enough in these old cottages.

He could picture Maddie standing at the sink, her straight blond hair brushing her shoulders as a breeze drifted in from the open window. Eyes as blue as the ocean gazing out at the sea. She'd probably have a little table in one corner, and he could picture himself sitting at it after finishing a home-cooked meal, maybe haddock or pasta or… whoa, wait a minute there. He and Maddie were cordial, but he doubted they would get friendly enough for her to cook him supper. What in the world was he thinking?

Lorelei would take a dim view of that. And he did not want to make Lorelei mad. She could make things very difficult when she was angry. But it wasn't always that way, was it? They'd known each other since high school but had only started dating a few years after college. Had it been almost ten years already?

There hadn't been any conflict at all in the early years. But relationships changed, right? And even though he wasn't head over heels about her like he had been in his youth, he still loved her and wanted to spend the rest of his life with her.

Maybe someday they could get a cottage on the beach like Starfish Cottage. Except Lorelei worked in Portsmouth, and she didn't seem to want to budge. In fact, she'd been getting downright aggressive about pushing Dex to move there with her. But Dex really didn't want to; he loved it here in Shell Cove. He knew the time was coming soon where he might have to make a hard decision.

CHAPTER THREE

*T*he Saltwater Sweet Shop smelled like heaven.

They'd been making chocolate there for so long, the delicious smell permeated every nook and cranny of the old store. Maddie was afraid that even just stepping inside would cause her to gain weight.

Of course, that might have been mostly due to the sea-salted caramels she was sampling.

"Gemma, my chocolatier, makes the best chocolates." Deena pushed the plate closer to Maddie. The creamy brown squares with their salt crystals called to her, and she took another one.

"These are so good," Maddie mumbled.

"They're Chuck's favorite." Deena looked over at the man arranging a shelf of nonpareils in the corner, her soft-brown eyes sparkling. He was tall, thin, and balding, but when he turned and winked at Deena, her cheeks flushed pink and she couldn't keep the smile off her face. It was adorable.

Deena had been widowed years ago and, according to Rose, had been in a depression until recently when she met Chuck. The two made a cute couple, and Maddie hoped things would work out.

Deena's gaze drifted from Chuck to the old recipe that lay on the counter. "I can't believe you found this in the old cottage. Did you know that we still use Etta's old recipes in many of our products?"

"I'd heard that." Maddie reached for the sample plate, this time picking a piece of penuche fudge. In for a penny, in for a pound. A pound that would go right to her hips.

"This one is interesting. Whisky fudge. It will make a very unusual addition to our offerings." Deena raised her brows.

"I was wondering if you know anything about Starfish Cottage? Did Etta own it?"

Deena frowned. "I'm not exactly sure. She ran the shop back in the twenties, I think. I don't remember anything about the cottage. Of course, that was before my time, and I think the family sold it. But I do think there was some sort of controversy tied into it. You know, the sort of thing that families like to keep secret."

"That's what I've heard." A secret controversy? Maddie hoped the place wasn't haunted or something.

Maybe there was a treasure to be found, as Dex had alluded to.

Deena turned to a table behind the counter. "We have these old photos from that time. I like to show them to customers because they show the early days of the candy store. It's been right in their building since day one, but was a much more scaled-down operation back then."

Maddie flipped through the pictures showing a woman in a 1920s sheath dress covered by a white apron. She was a pretty woman, petite, with her hair fashioned in the wavy curl popular at the time. Maddie recognized it as the same room they were in now by the placement of the doorway and tall windows, but the room was practically bare. A few tables with boxes of candy, and a large marble slab where the woman was cutting fudge.

They leafed through the photos with Deena making comments about some of them.

"That looks like my cottage!" Maddie pointed to an interior shot of a cottage. Etta was standing at the kitchen window, gazing out at the ocean. The kitchen cabinets looked new and freshly painted. Gingham curtains hung in the window, and a set of enamel canisters was lined up on the metal-trimmed Formica countertop. But even with the differences, Maddie recognized it as her kitchen.

Deena squinted at the photo. "I think there are

more from the cottage." She flipped to the next page, where Maddie got excited to see a picture of the dining room and living room. One bedroom shot showed a chenille bedspread and makeup table, Etta in a dark evening dress.

"Could I get copies of these?" Maddie asked. Even though it was definitely her cottage, there were a few differences, and seeing what it looked like originally might be helpful for her renovation. It would be kind of cool to get the pictures framed and hang them up in the house for nostalgia.

"Sure. I can make a copy right on my printer." Deena slipped the photos out carefully and disappeared into the back of the shop.

Maddie was eyeing a peppermint patty on the sample plate when the door opened and Constance Harbinger entered.

Maddie remembered meeting Constance at one of the town meetings. She was somewhat of a grouch then, and her demeanor hadn't changed, judging by the tight-lipped smile she gave Maddie.

Determined to be her usual cheery self, Maddie gave Constance a big smile. "Good morning! How are you?"

Constance looked surprised at Maddie's greeting. Maddie got the impression that not a lot of people greeted Constance Harbinger with a smile, and for a split second, she felt sorry for her.

"Fine, thanks." Constance clutched her purse to her chest as if expecting Maddie to grab it and run, and then disappeared behind a candy display without further comment.

She approached the counter with a bag of sour candies just as Deena was coming out from the back with the copies.

"Hi, Connie. I see you have the usual." Deena put the copies in front of Maddie and rang up Constance's purchase.

Constance—somehow Maddie couldn't think of her as Connie—avoided eye contact, keeping her gaze on the counter. Her eyes were fixated on the old recipe. "What's this?"

"An old recipe from my great-grandmother." Deena packaged up the sour candies in a white bag and handed them over. "Maddie owns Starfish Cottage now, and she found it in a drawer. Isn't that great?"

Constance snorted. "Whisky fudge? Sounds inappropriate. I hope you aren't going to add it to your selection of candies."

"As a matter of fact, I am. But don't worry. You couldn't eat enough of them to get drunk, so I don't think there are any licensing issues."

"Harrumph… I suppose if you say so." Constance took the bag and left.

After the door closed, Deena said, "She's kind of a sourpuss, but don't judge her too harshly. Her husband had a drinking problem and caused a fatal accident. She withdrew from society after that. Do you realize she's only fifty-eight?"

Maddie was shocked. "She looks almost eighty!"

"That's what a hard life full of bitterness will do." Deena shook her head. "She's practically a recluse now. The only thing she has is her work on the town approval committee, but with the lack of tourism, there hasn't been a lot for that committee to do."

"Hopefully that will change."

Deena smiled. "Thanks to you."

No pressure there. "Speaking of which, I'd better get back to work. Thanks for the copies of the photos."

CHAPTER FOUR

*M*addie took a deep breath as she pulled into the cottage driveway. Dex had wasted no time getting to work. He stood over a table made of sawhorses and plywood, cutting into a two-by-four. His tools were spread out haphazardly around the yard.

"Should have that doorframe repaired by the end of the day," he said as she stood there eyeing the mess.

"That's great. Thanks." Maddie smiled at him despite how much the untidy mess bothered her. She was going to have to ignore that for now. Dex was doing what she asked, and she needed the work done. The doorframe was so loose that locking the door wasn't much of a deterrent to anyone who wanted to break in.

"I'll start inside after that?" Dex asked. Maddie had wanted the interior work done first so that she could get started with the painting while Dex worked on the exterior. Frank had assured her that the cottage was solid, so there wasn't anything that was an emergency to be fixed right away. If she ran out of funds, it would bother her to have the inside in shambles more than the outside.

"Yes. Do you have a schedule of when you will start and complete each of the jobs?" Maddie had bought a separate day planner to use for the renovation schedule, but she hadn't filled it in yet because she wasn't sure how long each job would take.

"Schedule?" Dex made a face. "Not really. Some of the jobs do need to be done in a certain order, though."

"Right. So we can figure out how long each will take and schedule when the next one will start."

Dex made a face again. "That sounds like a lot of work."

"Not really. If you know where you're going to start and what order you'll do them in, at least we can estimate."

"That might be a little restrictive. I usually just move to the next job as I see fit at the time."

"You don't plan it by date? You just go with the flow?" Maddie wasn't surprised given what she knew about the way Dex worked from his jobs at the Beachcomber, but the thought of just going forward with no plan gave her anxiety.

"Renovations on old houses like this can't really be planned out exactly. Sometimes things come up that necessitate a change in plans, and I've found that can be disappointing to homeowners. How about we don't make a strict plan, see how it goes?" Dex looked at her as if he knew that the only thing worse for her than not having a plan was changing the plan they'd made.

She sighed. "Fine. I guess that could work."

Rose's car pulling in interrupted any further conversation.

Pearl Flannery jumped out of the passenger seat, a giant wicker basket loaded with food in her arms, and Leena McCain unfolded herself from the back with an agility that belied her age. "Welcome wagon!"

Maddie laughed. She'd met the energetic senior citizens who had been friends with her grandmother the first night she and her cousins had come to the Beachcomber. They'd arrived unannounced with a welcome wagon basket. Apparently they considered it their job to greet all newcomers, and since they'd been friends with Gram, they took special interest in Maddie and her cousins.

"I'm not exactly a newcomer." Maddie took the basket as Dex kissed Rose's cheek. Rose beamed, her blue eyes sparkling as she patted her halo of gray curly hair. The affection between grandmother and grandson was heartwarming and a sweet reminder of her relationship with her own grandmother.

Maddie brought the three ladies into the cottage

and gave them the short tour. "Have any of you been in here before?"

"I was many years ago." Leena stood in the living room and looked around, her hazel eyes assessing every detail. Shorter than the other two, she made up for it by spiking her short white hair up a bit on top. "It seems a little different."

"I think it had some work done over the years." Maddie had seen signs of more modern renovations, but she was hoping to restore as much of that as possible.

"I'm glad you're fixing it up." Pearl peered around the basket she was still holding, her white pixie cut making her look like a charming elf bearing gifts. "It's a great property and deserves to shine again."

Maddie relieved her of the basket and herded them toward the kitchen. "I couldn't have done it without you guys persuading Henry to loan me the money."

"That didn't take much persuading. Henry has really softened up. He's committed to seeing that Shell Cove thrives again, and part of that is making sure the properties are kept up."

"Henry's softening up might have something to do with a certain guest at the Beachcomber." Pearl's blue eyes sparkled mischievously.

"Aggie? I didn't know they'd become friends." Maddie set some of the cookies that had been included in her basket on a plate and took out some tea bags.

The basket was a welcome gift; she didn't have much on hand. She thanked the ladies as she unpacked boxes of tea, cereal, spaghetti, ketchup, and even some cleaning products.

"Aggie seems like a fun character. Maybe we should invite her for coffee," Pearl said.

"That's not a bad idea." Rose helped Maddie with the refreshments, and they all sat at the table.

"What's this?" Leena pointed to the copies of the pictures of the cottage that Maddie had gotten from Deena.

"I found an old recipe in one of the drawers." Maddie explained her trip to visit Deena and how she'd been kind enough to make copies of the photos. "She and Chuck seem so happy."

Leena nodded. "They do. It's nice to see that."

Rose patted her lips with a napkin. "Now let's talk about the event."

Maddie's spirits dimmed a tad.

"What are your ideas?" Leena looked at her expectantly.

Maddie reached for her notepad and flipped it open to a page with line items that were mostly crossed off. She'd brainstormed ideas but eliminated almost all of them.

"I was thinking we should tie it in to the beach. We have such a lovely beach here, and it's summer," Maddie said.

"Good idea."

"So, I thought maybe a sandcastle competition." Maddie looked at the three ladies hopefully.

Rose frowned. "Don't they have a big sandcastle competition in Old Orchard at the end of August?"

Pearl nodded. "Yes. I don't think we should do something that another town is having."

Okay, first idea shot down. Maddie ran her finger down the list. "How about an art fair? We could set tents up on the pier."

Leena shook her head. "Nope. They just had one in Ogunquit."

Maddie's stomach sank lower. "Okay, well what about a food event? Clam dig? Lobster bake?"

Rose poured more tea. "We just had the baking contest. I don't think we could top that."

"And there's a big lobster bake in several towns already. Nothing new there," Pearl said.

"I was thinking the restaurants and shops could show off their dishes." Maddie knew it was a weak idea, but she was basing her ideas on events she'd been to in other towns. Shell Cove didn't even have many restaurants.

"These sound like ideas that any town could have." Leena gestured toward the notebook. "We need something unique. Something people can't get anywhere else. Something people will drive out of their way for."

Maddie frowned down at the list. It was true. Everything she'd considered was so common. But how to come up with something unique that people couldn't get anywhere else?

Rose patted her arm. "Don't worry, dear. You'll think of something."

The ladies started clearing the table.

"Maybe something specific to Shell Cove," Leena suggested.

That was a good idea, but what? The only events Maddie knew of that towns were famous for were motorcycle rallies and landmarks. Rose, Pearl, and Leena had been in town their whole lives; maybe they knew something.

"Is Shell Cove famous for something? Maybe something that happened when you were kids or a famous person that lived here?"

The looked at each other but shook their heads.

"Can't think of anything off the top of my head," Pearl said.

"I know you'll figure it out. We have faith in you," Rose said as she loaded the last dish into the sink.

Maddie hugged the ladies and thanked them for the basket. Outside, Dex was unloading more tools. Hopefully he wouldn't leave them strewn about the yard as he'd done at the Beachcomber. Just the thought of it made her feel disorganized, and that was the last thing she needed right now.

She sat at the table and closed her eyes, trying to

come up with something unique. Wyoming had Long-mire Days after the TV and book series, but they didn't have a series associated here in Shell Cove. Sturgis, South Dakota, Laconia, New Hampshire, and Daytona, Florida had motorcycle rallies, but those events were on a tradition that had built over almost a hundred years.

Even Ariel, Washington had the unique distinction of being the area where the famed elusive hijacker D. B. Cooper parachuted over and had a festival in his name. What did Shell Cove have?

Her phone pinged with a message from Jules.

Wine at Beachcomber tonight? Gina made a chocolate cream pie….

With all the candy she'd eaten at Saltwater Sweets, Maddie really should decline. She thumbed in a text reply.

I'll be there at five!

Maybe wine and chocolate would help her think.

"I DON'T THINK SHE HAS ANY IDEAS FOR AN EVENT," Leena said back in Rose's car as they drove away from the cottage.

Pearl twisted in the passenger seat to look at her friend. It was Pearl's turn to ride shotgun, so Leena was in the back. "I agree. The cottage seems to be coming along, though."

"It sure does, but I thought Frank was going to be working on it." Leena gave Rose a pointed look.

Even though Rose was driving and couldn't see Leena, she grimaced. She knew what her old friend was getting at. "He's sick."

"Uh-huh." Leena settled back in the seat. "He seemed fine when I saw him this morning at Ocean Brew."

"Came on sudden," Rose said.

"Rose! Are you playing matchmaker?" Pearl asked. "You know Dex already has a girlfriend."

"I know, but don't you think he'd be cute with Maddie?" Rose asked. She didn't care much for Dex's girlfriend, Lorelei. She'd tried to like her because she wanted to be supportive of Dex. She wanted Dex to be happy, but the truth was she didn't think Lorelei would make Dex happy. She wanted Dex to move away to Portland, and she knew Dex would hate it there. Not to mention that if Dex moved away, Rose would be very unhappy. The two of them were close, and she'd miss him terribly.

"I think it's a good idea." Leena shoved a five-dollar bill over the back of the seat. "I'm putting five on them."

With not a lot to do in Shell Cove, the three ladies had taken to making small bets on things going on around town. Potential romances were their favorite.

Pearl took the money and shoved it into the glove box. "Don't forget you lost the Nules bet."

They'd also taken to combining the romance-interest names as a shortcut. Nules was Nick who worked in the bank and Maddie's cousin Jules.

"Not yet. I haven't seen anything official from them," Leena said.

"Young folks don't exactly send out announcements or wear the boy's pin like back in our day. They've been seen on various dates. I think you have to admit you were wrong and they are going to be a couple," Rose said.

Leena smiled. "Well, they do look happy together. Fine. You guys win."

"I'm not taking your bet on Maddie and Dex, though," Rose said.

"You mean Mex?" Pearl seemed pleased at her shortcut name for the couple. "Me either. We want them to get together."

"Well, that's no fun. Can't have a wager if we're all on the same side." Leena shoved her hand in between them and motioned for Pearl to return the bill. "I don't really care for Lorelei anyway, so I kind of do hope he ditches her and goes for Maddie."

"Yeah," Pearl agreed. "Dex is a sweetheart, and

Lorelei doesn't treat him very well. She's kind of bitchy."

Rose and Leena both looked at Pearl in surprise. She rarely used unkind words.

Pearl straightened her blouse. "What? She is."

"Can't argue there," Leena said. "Besides I think I might still be on to win the Chukeena bet."

"Chuck and Deena?" Rose asked. "There's no way those two are breaking up."

"I don't know. You said yourself their kids aren't for it."

"Hmm, true. They might have to stand up to them. They can't let their kids run their lives," Rose said.

"The kids don't even live in town. Deena's daughter doesn't know Chuck, and Chuck's son doesn't know Deena. They need to meet and give them a chance," Pearl said.

"Maybe we should suggest that," Rose said. "Now that we have a nice motel in town, the kids could come for a visit and see how happy their parents are together."

"Sounds like meddling. Maybe we'd better stay out of it," Leena said. "Besides, if Maddie doesn't come up with an event to bring people to town, we're going to have bigger things to worry about than other people's love lives."

CHAPTER FIVE

*M*aybe it was a silly thing, but Gina was proud to show off her chocolate cream pie to her cousins. She'd taken great pains on the presentation, and the dish was piled high with whipped cream sprinkled with shaved chocolate. Jules and Maddie both made a big deal of it, and they cut their pieces, grabbed a bottle of wine, and sat on the porch of the Beachcomber.

Life was strange, Gina mused as she rocked in her chair, eating the pie and looking out at the ocean as the sun set behind them, lighting the sky with pastel pinks and blues and glinting off the tops of the waves. When she'd first inherited the motel with her cousins, she hadn't even intended to stay in town. But now, she couldn't imagine being anywhere else.

Things had changed so much for her. She had a

place where she belonged and family that wanted her here. And possibly the start of a new career.

No sense in getting ahead of herself. Right now she was happy to get the approval of her cousins on each pie she made. Starting a business out of it could come later. Of course, she still had that little problem with her missing husband, Hugh, who had run off with his assistant and all their money. But the bigger problem was that the wave of tourists who had discovered Shell Cove from the baking contest was starting to dry up, and a lack of tourists meant no business for any of them.

"This pie is delicious." Maddie slid a forkful into her mouth and closed her eyes to savor it.

Gina still wasn't used to accepting compliments, especially after Hugh had made her feel worthless for their entire married life, so she quickly changed the subject. "Thanks. So tell us what you've come up with for the town event. I bet it's something even more exciting than the baking contest."

Maddie had lucked into the baking contest. She'd run into the producer of the *Great New England Baking Contest* in the local coffee shop. Their agreement with one of the coastal towns had fallen through, and they were looking for another town to host the contest in a hurry. Maddie had pulled it all together, and the contest itself and the show which aired the following week had been driving tourists to their struggling town.

Maddie's dreamy expression faltered. She put the plate aside and reached for her wine. "Well, that's the problem. It's going to be hard to top that contest."

"That did attract a lot of people." Jules glanced at the row of motel rooms adjacent to the porch. "But now reservations have tapered off."

"I know. I came up with some ideas and discussed them with Rose, Leena, and Pearl, but we need something big, and so far I've only come up with things that every town has. Sandcastle contest, food fairs…" Maddie sighed and leaned back in the rocker. "Do you guys have any ideas? Maybe something particular to the town that we can capitalize on?"

Gina's heart pinched at the hopeful look on Maddie's face. She wished she could help her cousin out, but Maddie was the best at thinking up great ideas and implementing them with all her day planners and schedules. Maybe she just needed more encouragement and less pressure. "You have the best ideas. I think you're putting too much pressure on yourself, and it's messing with your creative thinking."

"I do only have two days until I have to present something at the meeting. I have been researching things, and I just need something unique to tie to Shell Cove, a famous event or maybe a family."

"Maybe you should ask some of the people who have lived here for a long time. Don't Rose or Leena or Pearl know of anything?" Gina asked.

"Or Dex. I'm sure you have plenty of time to talk with him." Jules's tone was teasing. Gina smirked, finding it ironic that Dex had been the one working on Starfish Cottage when Maddie had made a huge point of hiring Frank.

Maddie focused on her wine. "Dex? I hardly see him. He's busy working. He still makes a mess."

Jules and Gina exchanged a look. It was no surprise that Maddie complained about how messy Dex was since she was so neat and orderly. Still, the two girls felt like maybe she complained a little *too* much, as if it were an excuse for her not to like him.

"He's a good carpenter," Jules said.

"True. He did a great job here at the motel," Gina added.

"Oh, I know. We just aren't buddies if that's what you guys are thinking," Maddie said. "I suppose it wouldn't hurt to ask him about town history though."

"Wine!" Aggie Fletcher came up the steps that led to the beach. She was in her late seventies and was always bright and bubbly. Tonight she wore a flame-red gauzy flowing top and had white slacks rolled up to her knees. Her feet were covered in sand, and she had a sand dollar in her hand.

"Would you like a glass?" Jules was already up from her seat, ready to fetch a wineglass.

"I'd love one, if you don't mind." Aggie sat in an empty chair. "I see you broke into the pie."

Aggie had popped into the kitchen while Gina was making it and oohed and ahhed over how it looked. Gina loved that Aggie was always quick with a compliment and encouraging words for her pie experiments, and since Aggie was a baking expert herself, those compliments and encouragement meant a lot. Gina cut a piece for Aggie and handed it over.

Aggie put the sand dollar down and dug in. "So delicious! You really are coming along and have quite a knack for this."

They settled back in their chairs as Aggie polished off the pie. "So what's going on? You girls look like you have something on your minds."

"Oh, it's just the town. We need to attract tourists." Maddie filled her in on how the contest had helped for a while, but now they needed something new and unique.

"Did you say you were looking for something to do with town history?" Aggie looked thoughtful. "I could ask Henry Barlowe. He's been around a while."

The girls laughed at her joke. Naturally, Henry had been around. He was over eighty.

"Where is Henry tonight?" Gina asked. Aggie hung around with him most nights, from what Gina could tell.

"He's down at that brewpub, Sharkies, I think it's called." Aggie looked at them as if wondering if they knew the place, and they nodded. Gina had only been there once, but she knew Jules and Nick had gone a few times. "He's with Nick. Grandpa-grandson bonding."

"Oh, so that explains why Jules is free tonight," Maddie teased.

Jules swatted her arm. "Hey! I don't spend *that* much time with Nick."

"You two do seem awfully close, dear." Aggie looked at Jules over the rim of the ruby-rimmed glasses that had slipped down her nose.

"We've only been on a handful of dates," Jules said.

"Well, it seems like you two get along really well," Aggie said. "But back to the problem. I hope Henry can help, and there are some other old-timers in town too. This town is just too adorable to give up on, and I'm sure once you start getting the flow of tourists, word of mouth will get out, and they'll keep coming. The motel is fabulous and the scenery gorgeous. Don't you girls worry. I'm sure it will all work out fine."

"You're probably right," Gina said. But she *was* worried. The three of them had a lot of hopes tied up in the success of the town. And if any of the old-timers —as Aggie called them—knew of something to base an event around, Rose, Leena, and Pearl would have mentioned something to Maddie before now. Still, she had all the faith in the world in her cousin, and she was determined to keep a positive outlook.

DEX WAS GLAD THAT SHARKIES WASN'T VERY CROWDED. The small pub could draw a crowd on weekends, but tonight only three people sat at the polished wooden bar, and all the other pub tables were empty. The brewpub was like a second home to Dex, the kind of place where everyone knew you, which wasn't really hard in Shell Cove since only locals ever came here. From the sports pennants behind the bar to the round pub tables to the warm lighting to the smell of burgers being cooked in back, it had a feeling of home.

Dex enjoyed talking to his best friend, Nick, and Nick's grandfather, Henry. When the bar was crowded, it was hard to hear what anyone was saying. Henry was getting up there in years, and Dex knew that shouting over the noise was an effort for him.

He'd been worried about Henry these past few years. The white-haired man had seemed to shrink into himself, shuffling along with his head down most of the time. But the past few weeks, Henry had changed. He had a spring in his step and a glint in his sharp, sapphire eyes. Nick did too, and Henry knew why. They both had new women in their lives. The change in his friends warmed his heart.

"So how many dates do you think is enough before I kiss her?" Henry was comically serious as he sat at the pub table across from Dex, his hand wrapped around a frosty mug of golden draft beer.

Dex shrugged. "Don't ask me. I've been dating

Lorelei since after college. Nick has more recent experience."

Nick beamed. Dex had noticed how happy his friend had been since Jules Whittier had come to town. It made sense; they were in those blissful days of a new relationship. Hopefully Nick would enjoy it. That feeling didn't last.

He was glad his relationship with Lorelei was stabilized, mature. None of that anxiety or second-guessing how the other person felt. Their relationship was predictable. It was safe. It was… not really that exciting anymore.

"I'd say two or three, Gramps," Nick said. "It sort of depends on what kind of dates they are."

"Maybe at your age you might want to speed up the timeline." Dex's joke brought a deep, genuine laugh from Henry. It was good to see him laugh like that. It had been a long time.

"Speaking of speeding up the timeline, I wanted to thank you for getting my garage repairs done so quickly." Henry's expression turned serious. "What do I owe you?"

Dex made a face and waved his hand. "There's never a charge for you, Henry."

The doors on Henrys two-car garage had rotted, and Dex had repaired them right away. He had no intentions of charging Henry for that work, though. Friends did that as a favor. Nick was his best friend, and therefore, Henry fell under that umbrella. Henry had a lot of money and could afford it, but that wasn't the point.

"No. No. Please, you're a young guy. You need money," Henry insisted.

"He's not that young." Nick laughed. They were both in their thirties. Though that might have seemed young to Henry, sometimes Dex felt ancient.

"Okay, well I won't be a pain about it, but I'm happy to pay," Henry said. "I get what you are saying. Neighbors take care of each other here in Shell Cove. Small-town life has its benefits, and you're important to the town. That's why I hope your young lady doesn't persuade you to move to the city. Rose said she was keen on it."

Dex's heart pinched. Though his grandmother always acted supportive, he knew she wasn't happy about Lorelei's recently ramped-up efforts to get him to move.

"You don't really want to move, do you?" Nick asked.

"Not really. I like it here." Dex didn't just like it, he *loved* it there. Lorelei said he wasn't adventurous enough to want to move from the town he'd lived his whole life in, but why move when you were already happy? Except Lorelei's escalating demands about moving were making him quite unhappy. She did have a point that since she lived in Portland and he lived here, they only got to see each other on weekends, but that had never bothered Dex. Maybe it should?

"I don't blame you. Everything I need is in Shell Cove. But you, if you want to settle down with Lorelei some day and start a family, you're going to have to make a choice about that," Nick said.

Dex frowned. He hadn't thought that far ahead. He was more of a live-for-the-moment guy than a planner.

"Don't tell me you haven't thought about that," Henry said.

"I haven't. I just kind of go with the flow." But now Dex *was* thinking about it. He loved Lorelei, but somehow the picture of them with a family wasn't jelling in his head.

"Speaking of planning." Nick nodded toward the window. Outside, Constance Harbinger strolled past the bar, glancing at her watch. She wore a yellow sweater draped over her shoulders despite the warm air and a scowl on her face.

"Drink up!" Harley, the owner of the bar, called out. His eyes tracked Constance from beneath bushy brows set in a frown as his beefy, tattooed arms worked at cleaning the bar with a kitchen towel.

The three of them sighed. Small towns were great for knowing everyone but maybe not so great for other things. Like old town ordinances and people that wanted to keep them intact. Somewhere along the line, Constance had resurrected an old ordinance from the

1930s that prohibited drinking after nine p.m. during the week as well as other strange town bylaws related to drinking. Even though it put a damper on some of the things Dex liked to do, he couldn't help but feel a pang of pity for the woman. She wasn't well-liked, and with good reason, but he knew it all stemmed from her husband's accident.

"At least it's only on weeknights." Dex drained his beer. It was time he got home anyway. He had a big day of work tomorrow at Shell Cottage, and he wanted to get an early start.

CHAPTER SIX

The next morning, Maddie sat on the back deck, her hand wrapped around a coffee mug as she gazed out at the ocean. The deck was one of the few things about Starfish Cottage that wasn't falling apart. It wasn't as old as the original cottage, and Maddie figured it had been added by the last owner, so it was probably about ten years old and in good condition.

With its spot right on the sand, it was the best space in the cottage and the only one with furniture other than an old bed she'd bought at a yard sale. Jules and Gina had helped her decorate the deck, and it boasted a cushioned wicker sectional, round outdoor rug, and cute shutters with starfish accents to match those on the cottage. Maddie had sprung for some flowering potted plants to add a pop of color. Jules had insisted on billowy sheer curtains. Maddie hadn't been sure about those at first, but it made the space seem like a private oasis on the beach where one could just relax and listen to the waves all day.

Maddie didn't have the luxury of listening to waves all day, though. She had her day planner out on the cushion next to her and a notebook handy so she could jot down ideas. She'd just crossed off the tenth idea in a row when she heard Dex's truck pull in.

Anxiety coiled in her chest. She found his mess distracting and his lack of schedule alarming. But she'd have to deal with it. She needed the cottage finished so she could focus, and since no good ideas were coming, she figured she should do what her grandmother had always advised her to do when she ran out of ideas—work with her hands and let her subconscious figure it out.

"I brought coffee!" Dex yelled from the kitchen.

At least he was thoughtful. She set her notebook aside and went inside.

"Thanks." Maddie took the coffee and looked around. Best to continue the sanding on the cabinets. That might occupy her mind so it could work on the event idea in the background.

"I'm waiting on some lumber to come in for the exterior. Do you want me to start on the walls today?" Dex asked.

The old wallpaper was peeling, and there were

water stains down the walls. Frank had told her it all had to be ripped down and skim coated (whatever that was) before it could be painted. But she had been thinking about taking some of the walls out to open the small cottage up. She'd love to get a view of the ocean in back from the living room that was in the front, but it would entail taking out the kitchen wall, and she was afraid it was holding up the top of the house.

"Sure. I might move things around, so maybe start at the outer walls."

"You got it."

Maddie picked through the sandpaper which she'd piled next to the electric sander.

"Are you sanding by hand?" Dex asked. "That's going to take forever. You have a sander right there."

"I know, but I like doing it by hand." Ugh… she sounded like a petulant child. She *didn't* like doing it by hand, but was embarrassed to admit that she couldn't figure out how to work the sander. Electronics and gadgets were not her strong suit. Gina had even had to help her with the old coffee machine when they'd first arrived at the motel.

Dex squatted down to look at the sander, his rumpled hair falling across his face.

Here it comes, Maddie thought, a condescending mansplain of how to use power tools.

But Dex wasn't condescending. "This model is a tough one. I used to have the same one and had a hard time figuring out how to put the sheets of sandpaper in. Let me show you a trick."

He brought the sander over, standing close while showing her how to place the front side in first then the back. "See how I doubled it up in the front? It seems to stay on better that way. Kept slipping off for me. What are you using it on?"

"The cabinets and drawers." They stepped into the kitchen, and she pointed where she'd already sanded the front of the drawer she'd found the recipe in by hand. "It will save me a lot of money to refinish them instead of getting new ones. I can do the work myself and paint them, and they'll be in keeping with the cottage style."

"Smart thinking." Dex's gaze fell on the picture she'd gotten from Deena. "What's this?"

"It's this cottage. Deena's grandmother lived here, I guess."

"Oh, right. The recipe." Dex's gaze skipped from the photograph to the wall. "That's weird."

"What?" She followed him around to the other side of the wall, which was in the living room.

"See how it's open in this picture? Looks like maybe 1930s or '40s when it was taken. They built the wall after that."

"Maybe they wanted the kitchen to be separate?" Maddie said.

"Maybe, but that's odd because the trend was

starting toward opening things up. Not closing them in. Pass-throughs were popular, but they didn't even do that with this wall."

Maddie glanced from the photo to the wall. It looked a lot better when it was open. "I wish they hadn't done it. I was thinking I wanted to take the wall down and open it up but was afraid it was there for a structural reason."

Dex glanced up at the ceiling. "Nope, it's not structural."

"So, it wouldn't hurt anything if we took this wall out?" Maddie asked.

"Not a thing." A smile spread across Dex's face as he turned to look at her. "You want to knock it down?"

"I was thinking it would be nice to put an island there and have it open. That way you could see out to the ocean from the living room."

Dex tilted his head and studied the wall. "Yeah, great idea. In fact…"

He walked over to the messy pile of tools in the corner, bent over, and picked up a sledgehammer. He turned it over in his hands. "I have just the tool, and I'm in the mood for some demo."

Panic bubbled up. "Whoa. I wasn't expecting to rush into it!"

"Why not? You said you thought about it already." He walked toward the wall.

"I haven't thought everything through yet. It needs

to be planned and… don't you need to draw up a blue-print or something?"

Dex laughed. "No. We're taking it down, not building it. Besides, you already know what it will look like from the picture."

Maddie glanced toward the picture. He had a point, but she wasn't used to acting on things so quickly.

"If you're going to tear this wall down, it's best to do it first. That way we'll know what we have to work with, and besides, it's always good to do the demo work first." He glanced eagerly from her to the wall.

"I suppose you're right, but I—"

Smash!

Apparently Dex had only heard the "I suppose you're right" part of her comment.

Maddie stared at the hole in the wall created by the tool. She turned to Dex, eyes wide. "You smashed a hole in it."

His smile faltered, concern rippling through his eyes. "I thought you agreed the demolition of the wall should be done first. I mean, you said I was right…"

Maddie took a deep breath, reminding herself that Dex wasn't exactly the type of person who thought things through. He was spontaneous, and he did have a point about tearing it down first. The demolition of the wall might bring up new ideas for the interior. "Yeah, I guess it should. I was just startled."

"I know you like to plan things out. We can wait for

a little while. I can peel the paper on the walls first, but that's only going to take a day."

"No, you're right. Let's get it done now. I'm kind of excited to see what it looks like."

"That's my girl! It's going to be a huge improvement." Dex lifted the sledgehammer up high, his shoulder muscles rippling under his T-shirt as he swung.

Smash!

Another big hole. Old horsehair plaster crumbled onto the floor in a pile, fine dust wafting out in a cloud.

"Maybe we should get a drop cloth," Maddie said.

"Nah. The floors need to be ripped up and replaced anyway, right?"

"Yeah, I suppose." She still didn't want a big mess.

"See? This is going to work out great. And it's fun." He grinned at her. "You want to try?"

"Me? I don't know how to demolish a wall." Maddie wasn't good with tools.

"It's easy. You'll really feel like you had a part in the renovation." He shoved the sledgehammer into her hands.

Maddie lifted the tool. It was heavy. If Dex swung tools like this all day, it was no wonder he had such big upper body muscles. Why was she thinking about that? She heaved it up and swung, practically falling over.

Plink.

Maddie stared at the tiny dent in the wall. "It didn't even break through."

"You have to really swing it. Think about something you are really mad about. Maybe me," Dex teased.

"You are a little irritating."

"So I've been told." Dex stood behind her and positioned the sledgehammer in her hands. "You hold it like this. Then pull back and really swing."

"Okay." Maddie closed her eyes, pulled back as he showed, and put all her might into swinging.

Crack!

That didn't sound right. Maddie opened her eyes. She'd made a hole in the wall, which was good. What wasn't good was that amber liquid was leaking out, and there was a pile of glass on the floor.

"What in the world?" Dex stared at the hole Maddie had made in the wall. Inside the hole was a broken bottle. He got closer and sniffed. Whisky?

Looking into the space, he saw that it wasn't just one bottle, either. "I think there's a stash of booze in here!"

"What?" Maddie peered in over his shoulder, her blond hair brushing against his arm, the lemony scent of her shampoo catching his breath.

His phone pinged. Probably Lorelei. Normally he answered right away, but what was happening right now with the whisky discovery and Maddie was more interesting.

They pulled away the rest of the wall to reveal a stash of twenty dust-covered bottles.

Dex held one up to the light. "Is it still good?"

"It looks really old. Check out the weird label." Maddie pointed to the paper label affixed to the bottle. It was the same on all of them. Yellowed and partially peeling off, it had what looked like a crown atop two letters, MR. "Is that some kind of whisky manufacturer?"

"I don't think so." Dex's phone pinged again, and he pulled it out. Another text from Lorelei, demanding to know why he hadn't answered the first one. It had only been a few minutes. When had she become this controlling? Maybe he shouldn't answer right away and give her the impression he was at her beck and call.

"Pearl mentioned something about a mystery connected with this cottage, and didn't you say that there was some rumor about a gangster living here?" Maddie asked.

"Do you think a bootlegger lived here?"

"The time frame people seem to be referencing fits with Prohibition." Maddie looked at the photo she'd gotten from Deena. "And this photo looks to be from the late 1920s or early 1930s."

"That was before the wall. Whoever MR is might have built the wall to hide his stash."

"Maybe. Doesn't exactly make it easily accessible, but maybe he had a good reason."

"This might be the thing I've been looking for." Maddie was bubbling over with excitement, and Dex could feel it too.

"You mean for the event to bring tourists to town?" Dex ignored the third insistent ping from his phone.

"Yes. Exactly."

"But we really don't know anything specific. Could you create an event around a bunch of whisky bottles hidden inside a wall?"

"No, you're right. I need to find out more." Maddie held up the photo. "And luckily I know exactly who to ask. If Deena's relative was involved, someone in the family might know something about this. Besides, I feel a craving for chocolate-covered Oreos coming on."

She turned and grabbed her purse, yelling over her shoulder, "You want anything from Saltwater Sweets?"

"No, thanks."

As Maddie drove off, Dex looked at the texts on his phone, each one ending with more exclamation points. He sighed and called Lorelei. It sounded like she was not happy with him. He was going to have to muster every ounce of charm he had to smooth things over.

CHAPTER SEVEN

*M*addie paused just inside the door of Saltwater Sweets and took a deep breath of the chocolate-spiced air.

Deena and Chuck stood at a table behind the counter, a river of melted chocolate spread on the marble surface in front of them.

"You have to keep it constantly in motion," Deena said as she used a wide metal spatula to spread the chocolate around. She handed the spatula to Chuck. "You try."

"Looks like fun," Maddie said.

Deena smiled. "It is. But it's also an art. Keeping it in motion, spreading and gathering helps stabilize the cocoa butter crystals. You're doing great, Chuck."

Chuck flushed at the praise. "It's kind of soothing, like a meditation."

Deena pulled off her black latex gloves. "When it gets a little thicker, put it back into the melter. I'll wait on Maddie."

Maddie tilted her cell phone up so Deena could see the picture she'd taken of the whisky bottles. "I was hoping to get some more information about Starfish Cottage. I found these in the wall."

"In the wall?" Deena took the phone. "Is that booze? I don't know anything about that. Do you think someone in my family put it there?"

"I'm not sure. It looks like there is a label. Maybe from the maker. Dex Wheeler—he's doing some work on the cottage—thought it might have been hidden by a bootlegger."

Deena's brows shot up. "How fascinating. I don't remember anything about a bootlegger in the family."

"Can I see the picture?" Chuck yelled. Apparently the chocolate had thickened enough for him to put it back in the melter, because the table had been scraped clean. He hadn't gotten all of it in the melter, though. He was wearing a good portion of it. His apron was smeared with chocolate, his hands were brown with it, and he even had some in his gray hair.

Deena laughed. "Maybe I should have showed you the technique to putting the chocolate back."

"No worries." Chuck licked a dab off his finger before pulling off his latex gloves and joining them at the counter. He tilted his head to see the image on the phone.

"I know what that is," he said.

"You do?" Maddie felt excited.

"Yeah." Chuck smiled as he slipped on a pair of reading glasses. "That's the signature mark for Marco Rosone. He was a famous bootlegger back in the twenties. You found these in the wall at the cottage?"

Maddie nodded.

"That's quite a find," Chuck said.

Deena beamed up at him proudly. "Chuck is a very successful historian."

"So, you know a lot about this bootlegger?" Maddie asked.

"Sure. He's kind of a cult figure in some circles. Was very flamboyant, and of course, there is a mystery revolving around him. He worked out of New York City, but the Feds were after him, and he disappeared. No one ever figured out where he went."

Visions of D. B. Cooper bubbled up. There were festivals about him. Maybe she could have a festival about Marco Rosone right here in the place he might have disappeared to while running from the Feds!

"Do you think he might have disappeared to Shell Cove?" Maddie asked.

Chuck shrugged. "Could be. How else would his whisky get in your walls?"

Maddie turned to Deena. "Do you remember your

family talking about a bootlegger?" Would she need more proof that he really did live in Shell Cottage in order to attract people to a town event?

Deena thought for a few seconds. "I vaguely remember some mention of parties back then. I never connected it with Prohibition, even though the talk was a bit hush-hush. No one ever mentioned a bootlegger in the family, but our family didn't sell the cottage until the 1970s, so I guess there must be some connection."

Chuck laughed. "Guess Etta Harper had more going on than just founding this chocolate shop."

"No kidding." Deena laughed. "I do remember hearing that she was a bit of a rabble-rouser."

"So what are you going to do with the whisky?" Chuck asked.

"I'm not sure. Seems like it could go in a museum or something. I was thinking though… if this guy is such a popular figure, maybe our next town event should be in honor of him." Maddie looked at Chuck. "Does he have a big following?"

"Oh, sure. That event in New York draws a big crowd. Of course, that might be because it's built around booze."

Deena frowned. "That might not fly so much here in Shell Cove."

But Maddie's head was already spinning with ideas. "We wouldn't have to focus on the booze. The 1920s and 30s are popular times. We could do something along that theme."

Now it was Chuck's turn to frown. "I think the people that like to follow him like the part about the booze, though."

"We could have that too." Maddie tapped her finger on the counter, already putting her advertising hat on even though the event hadn't been fleshed out or approved at the town meeting yet. "I wonder how we could get the word out to the fans of our famous bootlegger."

"Why not try the fan club?" Chuck said.

"He has a fan club?" Perfect!

"Yep. They have a website and are on Facebook."

"Thanks. You guys have been a lot of help."

"Are you really going to recommend an event around this bootlegger character?" Deena asked.

"I'm going to do some research and think it over. Of course, I need to find something that has broader appeal too. But if we make it a big celebration, we might just be able to attract a lot of tourists."

"That's a great idea. I could make those whisky chocolates from the recipe you found in the drawer." Deena's eyes gleamed.

"That would be fantastic! A recipe right from Marco's kitchen!"

Maddie took her chocolate-covered Oreos and left

with a smile on her face and visions of how she could present this at the town meeting whirling in her mind.

"WELL SHE CERTAINLY SEEMS ENTHUSIASTIC," CHUCK said as they watched Maddie leave.

"I like her attitude. This town has changed for the better since she and her cousins came to spruce up the Beachcomber." Deena pulled Chuck toward the melting chocolate. She was happier than she'd been in years and couldn't keep the smile off her face, and it felt good.

Chuck was a good man and determined to help her with the business. He was also wealthy, but that had nothing to do with how she felt about him. She'd turned down his many offers to invest in Saltwater Sweets. It was her family business and her responsibility to put it back on track.

She only wished her daughter, Samantha, would take the same interest in the shop. She was the only one Deena had to pass it on to, and she couldn't bear the thought of Saltwater Sweets not being in the family.

"They seem very sharp. It's great that she's planning an event." Chuck started setting the ingredients for the sea-salted caramels onto the worktable: caramel squares that they'd made earlier, coarse sea salt, and the various tools they needed for dipping.

"Sounds like it could be fun." Deena handed Chuck

the tongs. "Remember, dip the whole thing in, then twirl it around to get all sides coated."

"I know." Chuck smiled down at her. "And I won't forget to swirl the design into the top."

Deena laughed. She hoped she wasn't being too bossy. Chuck was a quick study and had a knack for chocolate making, as if he were meant to be here with her.

"If they do go ahead with the Marco Rosone theme, it could be good for Saltwater Sweets because your great-grandmother was associated with him."

Deena glanced at the recipe Maddie had given her. She'd put it in a protective plastic holder until she had time to take it to the framing store. She'd made a copy, but planned to hang the original recipe on the wall. "We haven't tried that whisky fudge recipe yet. Maybe this afternoon."

"Sounds good." Chuck placed the sea-salted caramel carefully onto the waxed paper. "I was thinking maybe we could do some special packaging to take advantage of that association. Maybe bags with 1930s-style printing. People love stuff like that, and they'd take the bags home and show them to their friends. Might bring in more business."

"That's a great idea." Chuck had been in marketing before and was always thinking up good ideas for her.

Deena felt hopeful for the future. With more tourists

coming to town and Chuck by her side, everything was perfect… well, almost everything.

As usual, Chuck sensed the shift in her mood.

"Is something wrong? Not enough salt on the tops?" He squinted at the row of sea-salted caramels, which were perfectly dipped and sprinkled with just a few grains of coarse sea salt.

"No, it's not that. You're doing a great job." Deena paused then decided she might as well confess her worries to him. "It's just that I told Sam about us, and she didn't seem very enthused."

Chuck frowned. Hopefully she hadn't hurt his feelings, so she quickly added, "I'm sure it's just because she doesn't know you."

"Oh, I wasn't taking it personally. In fact, my son, Cole, had the same reaction."

"Oh no." Deena felt like her happy bubble was about to burst.

"Honey, we're grown adults and can't let our kids rule our lives. They're also grown adults, and you'd think they'd be mature enough to be happy we found each other."

"I agree." Deena had been taken aback by Sam's obvious disapproval. Her only daughter was almost thirty, and Deena had expected a much different reaction. It wasn't as if she was replacing her late husband—he'd been gone for years—but that was exactly the way Sam had been acting. It was so disappointing.

"At least Audrey was happy for us," Chuck said about his daughter. He put his arm around Deena's shoulder and kissed her cheek. "We don't need our children's approval, you know."

"I know. But it would be nice to have it." Deena didn't want to lose Chuck, but if it meant being estranged from her daughter…

"Maybe we can come up with a way to get their approval? I'm sure if they knew how good we are for each other, they'd change their minds."

"What do you mean?" Deena asked.

"I'm not exactly sure, but there might be a way for us to *show* them how good we are together instead of just telling them." Chuck smiled down at her. "You let me think about that, and don't worry. Everything will work out."

CHAPTER EIGHT

"*Y*ou found whisky inside your wall?" Gina looked up from the apple pie she was slicing, her expression a bit incredulous.

After visiting Saltwater Sweets, Maddie had come straight to the Beachcomber to tell her cousins about the unique discovery. Gina had been baking, and the motel kitchen smelled of sugary dough and spiced apples.

The apple pie wasn't her only creation. Four other pies sat on the counter. Maddie wondered if maybe Gina was getting a bit overzealous with the pie making. There were only a few guests at the Beachcomber now. Who could eat all this pie?

"That's so cool. Nick was really excited about that." Jules was sitting at the table, going over the paperwork for the motel.

"Nick knows already?" They'd only made the discovery a few hours ago, and Maddie had only told Deena and Chuck. Then again, Dex and Nick were best friends. He'd probably called him right away. And judging by the way Jules was blushing, Nick had called her right after that.

"So that's the important phone call you had to take down to the beach earlier?" Gina winked at Maddie then handed them each a dessert plate with a slice of pie. Maddie was going to need a new wardrobe in a bigger size if Gina kept this up.

Jules apparently thought it was time to change the subject, because she said, "Tell us more about the whisky."

"Are you going to drink the whisky?" Gina shoved pie in her mouth.

Maddie made a face. "I'm not sure it's still good."

"Of course it is. Booze gets better with age," Gina said, licking some apple off her fork. "But I think the town should save it. Put it in a museum or something."

"I haven't actually thought much about what to do with the bottles." Hopefully the entire cottage wasn't full of moonshine bottles. Maddie didn't have room to store them, and now she was wondering if they even actually belonged to her.

"I heard that Harley down at Sharkies was going to store them," Jules said.

"Oh, I guess you know more than I do." Dex must

have called Harley too. Maddie didn't mind. She didn't really want to keep the whisky anyway, and Gina's idea of putting them on display was a good one. The town didn't have a museum that she knew of, but maybe it should.

"Sorry," Jules said. "Word gets around fast in a small town. And it's a pretty exciting discovery. It's cool that it was hidden in the wall all this time."

"And that a bootlegger lived in Shell Cove. Very exciting," Gina said.

"I'm hoping other people will think so, too, and want to come to the town to find out more." Maddie told them the details of how they'd discovered the whisky in the wall and what she'd learned about Marco Rosone so far. "I haven't thought it all out yet, but I want to take advantage of our gorgeous beach and the pier. Deena said she would make the whisky fudge recipe that I found in the drawer, and I was thinking maybe the other businesses in town might want to do something special related to the occasion."

"That's a great idea," Jules said. "We can show off the town and the great businesses to make people want to come back."

"I can make a bourbon pecan pie." Gina reached for the recipe box that held their grandmother's pie recipes. "I think Gram had a recipe in here."

"This bootlegger guy actually has a fan club, and they have an annual event, so he sort of has a following.

I'm going to do some research on him and come up with a plan that I can present at the town meeting." Maddie glanced at her watch. "Speaking of which, I better get going. The meeting is tomorrow night, and I have a lot to do."

Jules jumped up from her seat at the table. "Take a pie." She grabbed a pie from the counter and shoved it at Maddie.

"A whole pie? I can't eat a whole pie."

"Maybe Dex would like some." Jules shoved the pie closer.

"I don't know…" Maddie could actually eat half a pie in one sitting. It might not be a good idea to have one hanging around.

"Don't you like pumpkin? I thought it was one of your favorites." Gina's tone held a note of disappointment.

"Oh, it is…" She didn't want Gina to think she didn't like her pies. "I'd love to take it. Thanks!"

She took the pie from Jules. It was gorgeous with a perfectly fluted crust and little maple leaves cut out of crust and sprinkled with large granules of sugar placed artfully on the top.

"Here, take some whipped cream." Gina was all smiles now as she held out a small bowl with homemade cream. Clearly, Gina felt happy when people appreciated her pies, and that was worth a few extra pounds to Maddie.

"Thank you."

"I might make a pumpkin pie for the town meeting. What are you making?" Gina asked.

Shoot! Maddie had forgotten that signature dishes were practically required for the meeting. Rose had said it was the only way they could get people to show up. Since Maddie had lived at the Beachcomber for the previous town meetings, the three of them had brought one dish, but now that she lived on her own, apparently she would be expected to bring something of her own.

"Good question. I have no idea."

"Maybe you should just bring the whisky," Jules joked. "Then everyone would be in a good mood."

"Ha ha. I'm afraid some might not approve, but I'll have to think up something. As you guys know, my culinary skills are lacking."

"Don't worry, cuz. I'm sure you can whip up something, and even if you don't, will anyone notice? It's more important that you come up with a plan to put this town back on the map." Gina opened the door since Maddie's hands were full with the pie and the whipped cream.

Maddie drove home, only slightly worried about the dish for the meeting. Gina was right. The important thing was the presentation and getting everyone on board with her idea for the event. She had a good feeling that it was going to be a hit.

CHAPTER NINE

*M*addie loved the deck behind her cottage, but the ocean breeze, warm sun, and swooping gulls did make it a bit hard to focus on the timelines, flowcharts, and lists that she was making for her event proposal.

After leaving her cousins the night before, she'd talked to the head of the Marco Rosone fan club, and he'd been excited to verify the whisky bottles were Rosone's. He'd also given her some ideas for what the fans would want in an event. He was excited and promised to spread the word.

Maddie was thrilled about that. It was like free advertising. But she didn't want just the Marco Rosone fan club to come to Shell Cove. She wanted to attract as many tourists to Shell Cove as possible, so she needed to make sure the event also had broad appeal. And what was more broadly appealing than food, drink, and dancing on the beach?

"Gorgeous day." Dex had come around the side of the house and was looking toward the ocean, his gaze fixed out at the sea-green waves crashing onto the beach.

"It is! Makes it hard to keep my mind on work with this gorgeous setting." Should she invite him up to the deck? It wasn't like he was a friend. He was working there, but it felt awkward just leaving him standing there in the sand.

"Have you thought about what to do with the whisky?" Dex asked.

"I certainly can't drink it all," Maddie joked. "I'm not really even sure that it's mine."

Dex laughed. "I think it's yours. You own the house. My buddy Harley, down at Sharkies, said he could store it for you if you want."

"I heard."

Dex frowned. "You did?"

"Yeah. I talked to Jules. I guess she heard it from Nick."

"Oh yeah.. those two have become very close." Dex glanced out at the ocean again but not before Maddie saw a strange look in his eyes. Longing? Did he long for what Nick and Jules had? Maddie had to admit feeling a pang of longing a few times herself upon seeing how happy Jules was since she'd gotten together with Nick.

"He seems nice."

"He's a great guy. Don't worry. He'll treat your cousin really well."

"That's good to know. Okay, well I guess I don't need all that whisky hanging around the cottage, so it would be really helpful if Harley did take it." Maddie made a mental note to pop into Sharkies and thank Harley. She'd only been there once before, and she wanted to start patronizing the businesses in town anyway. "I don't want it to get ruined with the renovation going on, and I don't see a museum in town to hold it for a display or anything."

"There used to be a small one when I was a kid, but since tourists don't come anymore…" Dex let his words trail off, and Maddie sensed his regret at the declining state of the town.

"Hopefully we're going to fix that." Maddie made a mental note about the museum. Maybe once things picked up, she'd see about reviving it.

Dex glanced at the paperwork spread all over the settee. "Is that what you're working on?"

"Yes. I'm going to make a presentation at the town meeting. Do you want to see it?"

"Sure." Dex stepped onto the deck, and she gestured for him to sit, turning the paperwork in his direction.

"I figure we'd stretch the event over a weekend starting on Friday. I have a potential timeline of events that happen throughout the entire weekend. Then there is a list of local businesses that might want to set up a tent, and a map of the town and where each tent could be placed." Maddie was excited to show her ideas to someone. She pointed at each of the documents as she talked, her words tumbling out, hands gesturing animatedly. "I've only just started the list of supplies. Of course, then there's advertising and cleanup and porta potties and…"

Dex held his palms up. "Whoa. Sounds like you have a lot planned out, but maybe it's not such a good idea to have it so… detailed."

Maddie's excitement dimmed. Of course Dex would say that; he never planned a thing. "When you plan things thoroughly, it ensures that there are no last-minute surprises and everything runs smoothly. I think that's important." Did she sound childish?

"But what if something you didn't plan for comes up that doesn't fit in with your plans?" Dex had had that happen a few times in the past, which was one of the reasons he preferred to just go with the flow. The other reason was just that it was his easygoing nature. Maybe he shouldn't have said that, though. The look of hurt on Maddie's face had him regretting his words. "Look, I'm not saying it's bad to plan. It's just that sometimes if you get it stuck in your head that things should be a certain way, it makes it hard to pivot in a new direction."

Maddie chewed her bottom lip. He had a point, but surely she'd thought of everything. "I guess you have a point, but I think I need to have some of this for the town meeting. People are going to want to know the scope of the event, especially since we'll need money from the town budget."

"Of course. It's a great plan. And I love the map. It's important because we'll need to put up some structure and make sure the tents will fit."

She watched as Dex pointed out various spots on the map and talked about some of the pitfalls they might run into with traffic flow. She hadn't thought about that sort of thing, and his advice was welcome. He wasn't so bad, and now she had a feeling she might need his help. He seemed just as excited about the event as she was, and she got a sense that he really did love Shell Cove. She felt a friendship forming despite the fact that they were so different.

"Are you coming to the town meeting?" Maddie asked once they were done discussing the plans.

"Oh, I don't know. That's tonight? My girlfriend is coming back from Portland, and she usually doesn't like to go to the meetings." Dex glanced down at the plans. "But this is important to the town, and the town is important to me. I'll be there."

Right. Dex had a girlfriend. She'd already known

that. She was glad he was going to the meeting. He could help persuade people if they balked since he knew so much now. So why did she suddenly feel so disappointed?

CHAPTER TEN

*M*addie felt oddly nervous when she walked into the town hall for the meeting later that night. Glancing anxiously at the food table, she made her way to the front of the room with her laptop. She'd spent most of the day making cost analysis presentations, maps, and charts with her project management software and hadn't allowed any time for creating the signature dish for the meeting.

It was so unlike her to come unprepared, and she was a bit embarrassed that she'd only had time to dip some pretzels in chocolate and throw them on a plate. She'd tried to sneak in and quickly put the dish on the table without anyone noticing.

She took her seat, and Rose, Leena, and Pearl shot her encouraging smiles. That made her feel better.

Rose started the meeting, and they discussed a few

mundane points of town business before she announced that Maddie was going to present her idea for the next town event. Now all eyes were on her as she hooked her laptop up to the projector and prayed that it worked.

Her screen showed up on the wall, and she breathed a sigh of relief. She turned to the crowd. She'd only been in town a month, but already so many faces were familiar. Most of them were friendly. Her cousins were seated in the front, giving her the thumbs-up sign. Rose, Leena, and Pearl were on the edges of their seats, their faces eager.

Was that Dex in the back row? Her heart warmed knowing that he'd come even though he usually didn't attend the meetings. His expression was encouraging; the beautiful blonde next to him, not so much. That must be Lorelei. She was all long legs and cascading honey-blond hair. Maddie supposed her face was pretty when it wasn't set in a bored scowl like it was now.

She took a deep breath and started the speech she'd practiced for hours the night before.

"I'm sure you all know how wonderful it was to have a flood of tourists from the *Great New England Baking Contest.*"

People nodded and murmured and smiled.

"And I'm also sure you've noticed that flood is dwindling to a trickle."

People nodded again, their smiles fading now.

"Well, I want to open the floodgates again, and this time hopefully the tourists will keep coming."

People shifted in their seats, leaning forward with interest.

Maddie went through her whole presentation. From the idea for the festival to the interest she'd already received from the fan club to her ideas to expand that to appeal to broader interests. She showed the map of the locations in town that they could set up vendor tents and her ideas on what events and vendors might take part.

"I think many of the businesses here could have a tent. That way tourists coming will get introduced to your products as well as our beautiful town and will hopefully want to return for weekends and vacations."

Jules raised her hand, and Maddie nodded toward her.

"I was thinking we could offer special discounts and packages to bring people to the Beachcomber," Jules said. "Like discount getaway weekends. Maybe some of us could get together and offer packages."

"Great idea!" Rose said.

"I could add some coffee discount cards to the package. Buy one get one free," Cassie, from Ocean Brew, chimed in.

"And I could offer a discount on meals," Harley added.

Burt Hastings stood. "I could have a moonshine-making display complete with bathtub."

Everyone turned to look at him, and he blushed. "What? My grandfather taught me when I was a boy. It's not like I make moonshine at home myself anymore."

From the looks on people's faces, Maddie got the impression that maybe he did make it at home, and it wasn't much of a secret.

In the back row, an older, white-haired gentleman raised his hand. Dwight Ryder was somewhat of a killjoy and always had something grumpy to say. Maddie hated to call on him, but she did.

"How is all this going to get done? Sounds like it takes money, and this town doesn't have any."

"That's not entirely true," Pearl piped in. "The Baking Show paid a hefty fee for permits and such. We can use that money. Isn't that right, Belinda?"

Belinda Simms, who ran the town hall, nodded.

"Well, there's still a lot of work to do," Dwight persisted. "Is it that much money to pay for all the labor?"

"We can save by doing a lot ourselves. I'll be happy to spruce up the plants around town and help set up the tents. I'm not afraid of a little hard work." Lorna Baxter, who owned the landscaping business in town, was always eager to lend a hand. She happened to be sitting next to Dwight and elbowed him good-naturedly in the ribs. "What about you, Dwight?"

"Err... no. I guess I could help."

"Now that's the spirit!" Rose said.

"I'll help with any carpentry work, repairs, and setup that need to be done. Free of charge," Dex said, looking pleased to be lending a hand and oblivious to the angry look on Lorelei's face.

"Ahem!" Heads swiveled toward the back where Constance Harbinger was standing, a look of disapproval on her face. Speaking of a killjoy, she was worse than Dwight.

"It seems like this event is centered around alcohol." Her lips puckered in distaste.

"Well, Marco Rosone *was* a bootlegger," Maddie pointed out, feeling defensive. "And we do have a built-in audience for an event about him, but that's not all the event is about."

Constance lifted her chin. "Really? It seemed that way in your presentation."

She had a point, but Maddie wasn't going to let her spoil things. So what if it was mostly about booze? Then again, maybe that would be off-putting to some folks. She didn't want to attract only people who liked to drink to town and wanted a broader scope than just the Marco Rosone fan club.

"I have some other ideas that don't center around moonshine that I haven't fully worked out, so I didn't present them yet. I'm sure you'll be pleasantly surprised." Maddie would be surprised, too, because she didn't actually have any other ideas. She'd come up with something, though.

That seemed to placate Constance even though she still looked doubtful. "We'll see. The town bylaws are very strict about alcohol displays and availability. I'll have to consult them."

"I'm sure we don't want to break any of the town laws." Maddie looked around the room, which was suddenly very silent. "Any other questions?"

No one raised a hand.

"Okay, then I guess we should vote."

Rose was already out of her seat and replacing Maddie at the podium.

"I don't need to tell anyone here how important it is to bring tourists back to Shell Cove. I think Maddie has proposed a fun and unique event. So, without further ado, everyone in favor, raise your hand."

To Maddie's relief, a sea of hands went up.

Rose counted. "It's official. The event is on! We'll set up a committee to study the details and for review of the progress. Now, you can all go eat."

Chairs scraped back, and people raced each other to the food table.

Maddie unplugged her laptop with mixed feelings. She was glad the presentation had gone well and almost everyone was on board... everyone except Constance

Harbinger. But the event was good for the town. Surely Constance wouldn't do anything to get it shut down?

"This pie is delicious. How do you get the crust so flakey?" Cecily Swenson shoved another forkful of blueberry pie into her mouth and closed her eyes.

"And the presentation." Alma Stonely held her hand to her chest. "So divine!"

Gina beamed with pride. After Maddie had finished her presentation, people had made a beeline for the food table, and several had gone directly to Gina's pie.

She had to admit, the pie did look amazing. She'd made a fluted lattice for the top and sprigs of leaves made out of dough with blueberries in the center. It was the most attractive dish on the table even if she did say so herself.

Her gaze fell on the chocolate-dipped pretzels. Maddie had looked embarrassed when she'd dropped them on the table. Gina pretended to rearrange some of the dishes and slid the pretzels behind the triple-chocolate layer cake. She didn't need anyone making negative comments and bringing Maddie down.

Gina was starting to get a reputation for the pies, and it felt good to have created something that people appreciated. She hadn't felt that way in a long time, mostly due to her husband, Hugh, who had always made her feel like she couldn't do anything right. But that was in the past. No sense in wasting time thinking about Hugh now… except… she might need to think about him, if she wanted to give herself the best future that she deserved. But not right now. Right now she wanted to enjoy the moment. Maddie's presentation had been fantastic, and everyone in town seemed excited about it. She was positive things were going to work out for Shell Cove and her own future.

She smiled at Cecily. "The secret to flakey crust is in how you mix in the butter."

"Oh, do tell exactly how."

"I can't give away all my secrets," Gina teased.

Cecily and Alma laughed. "You are a treat! I'm so glad you girls moved to town."

Gina's heart expanded at the compliment. No one had ever said that to her in Boston.

"You really should start a bakery. We don't want to have to wait for another town meeting to get some of this pie." Cecily said.

"That's a great idea." Pearl had joined the group. She gave Gina a pointed look. "That old bakery shop in town is still empty."

Pearl had once pointed out an old store in town that had been a bakery and still had the equipment perfect for pie baking. Gina wasn't quite ready for that, but she was getting close.

"I have enough right now, practicing on the Beachcomber guests," Gina said.

"Speaking of which, Maddie's presentation was good. I think this event sounds fun," Rose said. She and Leena stood beside them with full plates.

"It does sound fun, but at least one person here didn't think so," Leena said before taking a bite of a deviled egg.

Rose made a face "Constance."

"I'm a little worried about her. Do you think she'll cause trouble?" Maddie leaned over Gina to get to the cream cheese brownies.

"Hopefully not," Pearl said.

"Don't be too sure. She's had a bee in her bonnet for years. Wouldn't surprise me if she doesn't even *want* the town to succeed," Leena said.

"I wouldn't be so harsh on her." Pearl gestured for them to move aside, and they all shuffled out of the way to make room for the others to get at the food. "She's had it hard since her husband died."

"That was a long time ago. People have tried to help." Leena didn't seem the least bit sympathetic.

Rose turned to Maddie. "I think if you just find something to add that doesn't focus on alcohol, she won't be able to find a reason to ruin things. You said you already have some things in mind. Let's hear them."

"Oh, well…" Maddie fiddled with the brownie on her plate.

"Maybe you shouldn't tell us until you have things worked out and finalized." Gina to the rescue. She had a feeling Maddie needed time to work through her ideas.

Maddie shot her a grateful smile. "Yes, exactly. I wouldn't want to talk about something that won't come to be."

"Well now, don't you worry about Constance. She's hardly the only grouchy one in the town." Rose's gaze drifted out the window, and Gina followed it to see Dex and Lorelei standing beside his truck. It looked like they were in a heated discussion.

Leena noticed too. "Trouble in paradise out there?"

"I was proud of Dex for volunteering." Rose's affection for her grandson was evident. "But maybe Lorelei isn't so keen on that."

"I heard her talking on the way out," Pearl said. "She seemed to think Dex's offer to help with the event will prevent him from spending more time with her in Portland."

"Indeed. Let's hope it does," Rose said.

"Rose!" Pearl feigned shock.

Rose shrugged. "I just don't think she's right for him." Her gaze shifted to Maddie, and Gina could practically read her mind. Interesting because Gina had always felt like Dex and Maddie would make a good couple. Apparently Rose had the same idea. And it was clear she didn't love Lorelei.

"Sometimes things just don't work out for couples." Deena and Chuck had joined them and were looking out the window at Dex and Lorelei now too.

"And sometimes couples find each other later in life. Like the two of you," Rose said.

Deena sighed and glanced at Chuck. They both looked depressed.

"Is something wrong?" Rose asked.

"It's our kids again. They're really starting to get us down. They simply won't listen to reason." Deena gave a sad smile. "But I don't want to bring down the mood. I have something Maddie might want to look at."

Maddie looked interested. "Oh, what's that?"

"I found an old trunk with some of Great-grandma Etta's things in them. I thought since you own the cottage now you might like to look through them."

"I'd love that. Are there more pictures of the cottage?"

"A few but just exteriors. No whisky or mention of it." Deena laughed.

"It still will be fun to look, and who knows, maybe it will give me some ideas for the Marco Rosone event."

"Excellent. I brought it over to Saltwater Sweets, so just stop by whenever you have a chance." Deena turned to Gina. "And Gina, I must compliment you on that pie. It was so delicious. I was a big fan of your grandmother's pie, but I think you might have outdone her."

"Really? Thanks." It was the best compliment Gina had ever received. Maybe it was time she gave more serious consideration into taking that next step.

DEX STARED AT LORELEI IN CONFUSION. WHEN HAD this selfish side of her emerged? Had it been there all along and he never noticed, or maybe it had never been tested?

"I just don't see why you have to volunteer to help. There are plenty of other guys in Shell Cove who can do that. What am I supposed to do while you are tied here to this town?"

Dex didn't know how to reply. Was this the same woman he'd known since high school? Because right now, the way she was standing with her arms crossed over her chest and her usually pretty face twisted into a grimace, she seemed like a stranger.

"I only want to help the town. You know how important Shell Cove is to me."

Something flickered across her eyes. Anger? Jealousy? Dex couldn't be sure. He was too shocked at her reaction. She was totally overreacting.

"Why? You have to admit, there's not much here." Her expression softened, and she dropped her arms and stepped closer to him. "And you're going to be leaving and moving in with me soon, aren't you?"

"Soon?" This wasn't the first time she'd asked, and the requests had been getting more frequent. Dex hadn't put much thought into it, though. He wasn't very excited about the idea, and he also didn't like to plan too far ahead. But Lorelei's job was in Portsmouth, and it was too far to commute from Shell Cove. And, as she'd pointed out many times, he could do carpentry anywhere.

But the thought of leaving his beautiful hometown by the sea made his heart ache.

"What are we waiting for?" Lorelei's voice was as smooth as honey now. The hard edge it held just moments ago was gone. "I thought we talked about this."

More like *she* talked and Dex avoided. "I know, but things are going good for me in town now. There are a lot of new opportunities, and I want to take advantage of that."

"So now you're rethinking about moving to Portland? Because if you are, that could be a deal breaker."

The look of disappointment on her face broke his heart. He didn't want to disappoint her, but then he thought of his grandmother and how disappointed *she* would be if he did move. He didn't want to disappoint her either.

Panic bubbled up in his chest. Lorelei was putting

him on the spot, and he didn't do well with being put on the spot. If not moving to Portland meant they would break up, then he certainly didn't want that. For almost a decade now, he'd had it in his head they would be together forever. He'd just never thought far enough ahead to envision what that would actually mean.

He didn't want to think about it now, either. He needed more time to give it his full attention.

"Of course not. I just don't want to rush into anything." He put his hands on her shoulders and kissed her forehead. She melted in and gave him a hug.

"Okay. Can we go out to eat now?" she said against his chest.

Dex had promised to take her to a fancy restaurant a few towns over if she came to the town meeting with him. "Yes. I'm starving."

He opened the passenger door for her, and she got in. As he walked around to the driver side, his mood lightened. The argument was over, at least for now. But sooner or later he knew he was going to have to make a decision.

CHAPTER ELEVEN

The next morning, Maddie awoke feeling both excited and worried. The event had been green-lighted at the town meeting, and she was excited to plan it out. But Constance Harbinger's subtle threat loomed over her. She needed to figure something out so that Constance wouldn't try to ruin the event.

She made coffee, booked advertising in some local papers, and started thinking about the logistics of the event. How many tents would they need? Would there be specific demonstrations or events? Burt had already mentioned the moonshine demonstration. Would they have other events too?

Most importantly though, she wanted to show off what Shell Cove had to offer, and that meant putting the businesses and the town scenery front and center.

She was elbow deep in paperwork and planning

when Dex showed up for work. He'd taken all the whisky to Sharkies and was planning on finishing the removal of the wall today. He'd brought her favorite latte from Ocean Brew.

"Thanks so much. My K-Cups aren't nearly as good." Maddie accepted the coffee gratefully.

"What in the world is going on here?" He raised a brow toward the papers that were spread out all over the kitchen counter.

"I'm planning." She pointed toward one of the papers. "I drew a model of the town and the shops. I'm figuring out where to put tents because we don't want to block the fronts of the shops, and you pointed out the problems with traffic flow in my original drawing the other day. And, of course, we want them to be able to see the pier and the beach and the ocean from as many places as possible."

"I should have known." Dex smiled. "But sometimes planning things on paper isn't the best idea. There might be obstacles in real life that you don't know about. Why don't we go downtown and look at what we have to work with? That way we can see any pitfalls there might be."

Maddie had the idea in her head that she could just work things out on paper, but Dex had a point. He was probably a lot better at these sorts of things than she was. "Okay. I appreciate the offer. I have to go to Saltwater Sweets anyway, so let's take separate cars and meet down there."

"Sounds like a plan."

It took less than five minutes to get from Maddie's cottage to downtown. Dex had parked in front of Salt-water Sweets, and she pulled in behind him.

They walked down the Main Street with her map, and Dex pointed out several things that had her adjusting her plan. Some areas weren't level, so she moved the tents to a more level spot. She hadn't accounted for the giant elm trees that lined the street either. Dex had some good ideas for placement, and she appreciated that.

"How many tents are there going to be?" Dex asked, glancing down the street to the ocean. "Too many will block the view."

"I'm not exactly sure. I asked the different shop owners to sign up if they wanted one, and the president of the Marco Rosone fan club suggested some out-of-town vendors they always have at their events."

"Let's not forget that we need a tent front and center for Burt and his moonshine demonstration."

Maddie and Dex both laughed, but then Maddie turned serious.

"I don't know. Constance Harbinger might shut him down on that," Maddie said.

"She did seem like she might cause trouble. I don't

know why she's so angry. Don't worry though. The rest of the town is behind you."

Maddie beamed. It felt good knowing that her newly adopted town and a friend like Dex had her back.

"Okay, well, I guess that's it. I better get back to the cottage. I'm hoping to finish that wall by the end of the day." Dex started toward his truck.

"That would be awesome. I can't wait to see what that looks like."

"Hopefully no more surprises."

"Let's hope."

Dex got into his truck, and Maddie opened the door to Saltwater Sweets, excited to see what was in Etta Harper's trunk.

THE DUSTY OLD TRUNK SAT IN THE BACK ROOM OF Saltwater Sweets amongst the chocolate-making supplies and ingredients.

"It's kind of moldy inside, but I thought you might be interested." Deena gestured toward the dome-top trunk. It was black with wooden slats across the top. The wood, probably once a honey-oak color, was now dull and dry with age. One of the rusted hinges hung askew on the back. Maddie opened it, and the scent of decades of dust wafted out and tickled her nose.

There wasn't much inside. An old Bible, some

perfume bottles whose contents had long evaporated, and a heap of fabric.

"Check this out." Deena lifted the fabric carefully.

The silky dress was probably once gorgeous. It was a sheath dress, the kind that hung straight down the sides and was the fashion in the 1920s and '30s. The green color had faded, and the beads along the bodice were falling off, but Maddie could see that it had once been a showstopper. She touched it gently. "The work on this is exquisite."

"I know. Too bad it's falling apart." Deena laid it gently to the side and pulled out a beaded purse full of moth holes. The green color and beadwork matched the dress, and the silver frame was etched with a scene of birds and flowers.

"Etta had some nice things," Maddie said. She was a little disappointed there was no diary or paperwork. She was hoping to find some information about Marco Rosone.

"I think she was quite the partier." Deena pulled out a long, tortoiseshell cigarette holder with a silver tip.

"I'll bet. Probably had a great time at Starfish Cottage." Maddie smiled, picturing big parties at her little cottage on the beach. Women dressed in flapper dresses, men in suits with hats. Bootleg whisky flowing. It was like something out of *The Great Gatsby*.

Wait! A Great Gatsby party!

"Well, I'm sorry there isn't really much in here. I

was hoping to find out something about her relationship with Marco Rosone. Like did he live there with her, or did she just hide his booze?" Deena laughed. "Guess we won't know from this trunk. I was kind of hoping it might turn up something we can use for the event."

Maddie hardly heard her. Her mind was whirling with ideas. Jazz bands, costumes, Art Deco-era decorations, all under the stars on the pier. "No need to apologize. Actually, this gave me a great idea."

"It did?"

"You know how Constance didn't approve of the focus being on Marco's reputation as a bootlegger?"

Deena made a face. "She doesn't approve of much."

Maddie pointed to the dress. "This could be the solution. We can have a Great Gatsby-style party. That will take the focus off moonshine but still be true to the era."

"That's a great idea!" Deena's eyes shone. "We can dress up in costumes. It will be fun."

Chuck had come over to stand beside Deena, and he looked excited too. "That does sound fun. I could break out my wing-tip shoes."

"And it's unique and will hopefully attract a lot of people." Maddie helped Deena put the things back in the trunk. She was bursting with energy to get back to the cottage and start planning. "I can't thank you enough for showing me the trunk. The party idea is a real lifesaver. If I can ever repay you, let me know."

Deena and Chuck exchanged a glance.

"Well, there is one thing," Deena said.

"What?"

"Could we get a discount on a couple of rooms at the Beachcomber? I wouldn't ask, but Jules said she was going to offer one, and we want to invite our kids to town." Chuck put his arm around Deena's shoulders. "We want them to see how happy we are together so they'll finally approve of our relationship."

"We'd be happy to give you a discount. No problem."

CHAPTER TWELVE

$\mathcal{P}$earl, Leena, and Rose were sitting on the bench across from Saltwater Sweets having an ice cream when Maddie came out.

"She looks excited. I bet she has an idea for the event," Pearl said.

"Deena and Chuck look happy too. They must have asked about the motel discount." At the town meeting after seeing them so unhappy, Rose had suggested they bring the kids here and *show* them how they were made for each other. Chuck had mentioned he'd had the exact same idea, so with both of them suggesting it, it seemed like a wise course of action.

"The kids coming could make things worse," Leena said. "I might still win the Chukeena bet."

"Did someone say 'bet'?" Aggie had come up behind them. She was wearing a turquoise tunic over white capri pants and had a chocolate chip cone in her hand. The turquoise color complemented her flame-red hair. She had a vitality about her, and Rose could see why Henry was spending so much time with her.

"Uhh... did we say bet?" Leena looked at Rose, uncertain if they should tell Aggie about their betting hobby.

"Yeah, you said..." Aggie looked across the street to Saltwater Sweets. "Oh, I get it. You guys are betting on the romance over there. They were telling me how their kids are acting like spoiled brats. The bet sounds fun. I want in."

"You do?" Pearl glanced at Rose as if for permission to let her join. Rose glanced at Leena, who shrugged. Why not let her join? Rose liked Aggie, and the more the merrier. Plus the pot would be bigger.

"Sure. We're betting five. Right now it's two for and one against."

She juggled the cone as she pulled a five-dollar bill out of her purse. "Put me down for against."

"You don't think they'll last?" Rose took the bill and stuffed it in the side pocket of her purse, making a mental note to add it to the betting pot later.

"I know it sounds mean, but adult children can be brutal. I have a nosy one myself. Always thinking he knows what's best for me. If they have it in their heads that Chuck and Deena aren't good for each other, it's going to be hard to dissuade them." Aggie licked the side of her cone. "That's why I don't mention Henry to my son."

Rose's brow ticked up. "And just what is going on with you and Henry?"

Aggie blushed. "We've hit it off."

"That's great," Pearl said. "We've noticed Henry is a lot happier these days."

Leena narrowed her eyes at Aggie. "Henry is our friend, and we want him to stay happy. So how long do you plan to stay in town?"

Aggie looked put off at first, but then she smiled. "Oh, I see. You don't want me to run off and hurt your friend. Let's just say I have no plans to leave anytime soon. The girls treat me like a queen over at the Beachcomber, and I want to see where this goes with Henry."

Leena smiled, scooted over, and patted the seat beside her. "Then why don't you have a seat and chat with us? Any friend of Henry is a friend of ours."

CHAPTER THIRTEEN

*M*addie rushed over to the Beachcomber to tell Jules and Gina about her idea for the party. She found them on the porch, and she plopped into a wicker rocker and gazed out at the ocean as she told them about looking through the trunk at Deena's and how it had seeded the idea of a Great Gatsby-style party.

"That sounds like fun. We could get it catered and have appetizers and maybe even some cocktails that were popular in that era," Jules said.

"What happened to the whisky that was in your wall? Maybe that would be a good time to break it open," Gina suggested.

"It might. Seems a shame, though. Does it have historical significance or something?" Maddie asked.

"Harley is storing it down at Sharkies, which reminds me, I need to stop down and thank him."

"Oh, perfect. You can meet me there tonight. I'm meeting Nick, and you've been working so hard, you need a break. You've hardly spent any time with us like Gina has, and I want both of you to get to know him better."

Maddie could hardly refuse. Her cousin wanted her to be a part of her life, and she was flattered. If Nick had been coming to the motel or hanging out with Jules and Gina, things must be getting serious.

Besides, she *had* been working hard and could use a little break.

"Okay, what time?"

"Six. We usually just split a few appetizers."

"Sounds perfect. Have we gotten any new reservations?" The event planning had taken up all of Maddie's time, and she hadn't been paying attention to the goings-on at the Beachcomber. "Sorry I haven't been around to help out."

Gina held up her hand. "No need to apologize. There's not much going on. We're down to just Aggie and no new reservations."

"I'm sure that will change once we start advertising the event," Jules said.

"The ads should start showing soon, and I put flyers up around town. Some local television stations might come out and report on the event. The committee meeting is tomorrow night, and I have all the ads ready to go. I just need the approval." Rose had formed a committee right after the meeting and asked Maddie to come up with final plans to present, and then they would vote.

"It's all good. Gives us time for some repairs," Jules said. "Speaking of which, how are things going at the cottage?"

"I haven't had time to do much myself, and Dex was helping me figure out where to set the tents and displays downtown, so there hasn't been much progress. He was going to finish removing the whisky wall today. I can't wait to see the ocean through the kitchen as soon as I walk in."

"That's going to be amazing. We can't wait to see it either," Gina said.

"After this week, I'll have more free time. We'll have a get-together." Maddie felt guilty that she'd neglected her cousins. "I should get going. I need to work up some ideas about the Gatsby party for the committee."

Maddie stood and took one last look at the ocean. Even though she could work on her back deck, she'd be much too busy focusing on that to look at the scenery. "See you at Sharkies at six."

Maddie opened the door to Starfish Cottage and gasped. Dex had removed the wall, and even though there was debris everywhere, all she could see was the aqua ocean vista through the window over the sink that was in the direct line of sight as soon as you entered.

Could the window be enlarged? She'd have to remove the cabinets on either side of it, but opening up that window would add a lot of light and more of the view. Maybe she could put a pantry cabinet in the dining room to make up for the lost space. But that would have to come in the future. She didn't have the money for that kind of renovation as it would entail a new window and probably some juggling of the existing cabinets.

"I'll just be happy with what I have," she said to no one because Dex wasn't there. The cottage felt a bit empty, but she needed the alone time to focus on her work anyway. She took a notebook and her iPad out to the deck and started to outline her ideas for the party.

By five p.m., she'd pretty much finished the plan and printed out some handouts for the meeting. Now, it was time for a much-deserved break.

It was a weeknight, so Sharkies wasn't crowded. She spotted Jules and Nick at a high-top table near the window and headed over.

"Hey, how's it going?" Jules gestured toward a chair opposite her. Jules and Nick both had mugs of beer, but there was a third mug on the table too. Had they ordered for her?

From behind her she heard, "Sorry guys. I got caught up talking to Harley... oh, hi, Maddie."

Dex took the seat with the beer in front of it. He was here too? She looked quizzically at Jules, who shrugged. Dex and Nick were best friends, so she supposed it stood to reason that Dex would happen upon them and join them. Strange coincidence... or was it? Judging by the guilty look on Jules's face, it might not be.

"Are you going to join us?" Dex asked. "Sorry I wasn't at the cottage. I had another job to go to, but what do you think of the wall?"

"It looks amazing." Maddie described how it had opened up the cottage to Jules and ordered a local IPA from the waitress.

"I'm so glad the place is coming together," Jules said. "What about the plan for the party?"

"That's coming together too." Maddie was pleased with the progress she'd made.

"Party?" Dex asked.

Maddie told Dex how the clothing in Deena's trunk had given her the idea.

"That's a great idea, and maybe it will keep you-know-who from being down on the event because of the association with spirits." Nick lifted his mug to emphasize the spirits part.

Harley came over to the table. He was tall, his slightly graying hair in a buzz cut and a white bar towel slung over his wide shoulders. "I hope you guys are enjoying the beer."

"You know it," Nick said.

"Harley, I've been meaning to thank you for storing the Marco Rosone whisky." Maddie smiled up at the man.

"No problem. I'm happy to help out. It's downstairs where I keep the kegs, anytime you want it."

"What are you going to do with it?" Nick asked.

"I was thinking maybe give it to the museum. I know it's not open now, but if the town blossoms like I think it's going to, we could get that up and running again," Maddie said.

"And you could make a display and use some of the items from Deena's trunk, if she'll let you," Jules suggested.

"That's a great idea. Shell Cove's most infamous resident," Maddie said. "Maybe we could make the Marco Rosone event a yearly thing."

"It does sound fun," Dex said. "What's the party going to be like?"

Maddie told them how she'd researched caterers so they could have some light food and even found a costume store that would come to Shell Cove and set up in one of the empty stores so anyone in town, including tourists, would have easy access to costumes. "I'll have to get approval from the committee for that, but some of those stores have nothing in them, and the costume people said it would be easy for them to set up racks."

"I love the idea of dressing up." Jules looked at Nick. "I bet you'd look great in a pinstripe suit and gangster hat."

Nick smiled at her and then steered the conversation in another direction. "You're doing a great job on the event planning, Maddie. Everyone in town really appreciates it, especially me and Gramps."

Maddie's heart swelled. She wanted Shell Cove to succeed because of the motel and her cottage, but it pleased her to know that people appreciated her work.

"And I'm glad you guys are working together on the cottage and the event setup." Jules raised her mug to them. "When you first started at the motel, I didn't think I'd see you guys ever get along."

Maddie glanced at Dex. Jules was right. At first, she'd thought Dex was too annoying to ever be friends with, but now she was getting used to him. Surprisingly she'd found him to be very helpful with the event too.

"It's a minor miracle. We don't actually have the same mode of operation." Dex's eyes twinkled at her over the rim of his beer.

"That's true, but you guys do have some things in common," Jules said.

"We do?"

Jules nodded. "You both have a good work ethic."

"And you both care enough about Shell Cove to go the extra mile," Nick added. "Besides, sometimes it's better if you have different ways of approaching the job."

Jules's gaze shifted to the window, and her brows drew together slightly. Maddie turned to see that someone had stopped outside and was peering in. It was Lorelei. Her gaze scanned the bar then stopped at their table. Dex's back was to the window, but she clearly recognized him, and then her gaze settled on Maddie. Her eyes narrowed, and her lips turned down.

"I think someone is looking for you." Maddie poked Dex's arm and then nodded toward the window.

Dex turned. "Oh. I guess she got in early. I gotta run." He stood and threw some bills on the table. "See you guys later."

They watched him rush out and greet Lorelei on the sidewalk. The two walked away hand in hand, and Maddie turned back to Nick and Jules. "Doesn't she like beer?"

"Nope. She's more the fancy-cocktail-bar type," Nick said.

"Really?" Maddie sipped her beer and glanced out the window again. "Doesn't seem like Dex is that type."

"He isn't, but I guess somehow it works for them."

"Does it?" Jules asked. "I mean, they don't seem very happy."

Nick shrugged. "They've been together forever, so I guess I stopped noticing. I *think* it works for them."

"I'm sure it does." Maddie turned her attention back to the table and Jules and Nick, but she caught herself wondering if things really did work with Dex and Lorelei. She'd sensed a bit of tension between them, but it was none of her business. She had more important things to worry about.

CHAPTER FOURTEEN

*M*addie worked all the next day gathering information on the party idea for the committee meeting. Dex was busy around the house, finishing up the wall, and then he moved to the exterior.

She sat on the back deck, so they really didn't have a chance to talk. She felt a little awkward about the way Lorelei had peered through the window at them the night before. She didn't want Dex to get into trouble with his girlfriend, but she also kind of missed talking to him.

The committee met in a small room in the town hall. Metal folding chairs were arranged around a long table. Rose, Lorna Baxter, Belinda Simms, Alice, and Constance were already there when Maddie arrived. She handed a stack of papers to each of them and told them about her ideas. To her relief, everyone seemed excited, especially about the Great Gatsby party.

"We could make it really festive and hang party lights, and I can place giant ferns in the corner of the tent," Lorna said.

"My cousin plays in a jazz band. I could see if we can book them. I'm sure he'd give us a discount," Belinda Simms offered.

"I think the owners will let us use the old donut shop for cooking the appetizers, and maybe we could even set up some tables inside," Alice Cunningham suggested.

"Okay, good. It sounds like the event is a go, then?" Maddie glanced hopefully at Constance, who was seated at the end of the table, her mouth set in a thin line. She hadn't said a word the entire time, and Maddie was apprehensive about the large blue binder she had in front of her.

"I do think the party is at least something that doesn't focus totally on drinking." Constance flipped open the binder. "However, from your diagram on the merchants, events, and layout of the entire thing, I believe there are several bylaw violations."

Everyone fidgeted in their seats.

"Oh? Which ones? Maybe we can change things to comply," Maddie said hopefully. She was willing to work with Constance to get the approval, but she couldn't change the entire theme of the event. Rosone's fan club was expecting certain things.

Constance started flipping through the book. "Section five, article A states that no obstructions should be placed in front of the town businesses." She gestured toward the sketches Maddie had made with vendor tents lining the sidewalks to show what the town might look like that day. "You clearly have tents in front of the businesses."

"Oh, good point." Maddie supposed the town fore-fathers might have been on to something with that one. People would want others to see their storefronts and go into the stores.

"Maybe we could put the tents in the grassy common area," Belinda suggested.

"That's a great idea," Rose chimed in. "We'll set them up so that when people come out of the shops, they see the fronts of the tents. That way they might see a display they want to check out."

"That will work perfectly." Maddie tried to adjust her mental picture of the event and looked over at Constance. "Is that it?"

Constance shook her head. "No. Article ten, subset four states that any public event needs to include the correct facilities. I don't see any accommodations for toileting."

That was no problem. "I did think about that and have a call in to Johnson's Porta Potties. I don't have a quote yet, and I didn't draw them in because I couldn't find a good place to put them. But now that we've moved the tents to the common area, that solves the problem of where to put them. If we line the tents up facing the shops, we can put the porta potties behind the tents. They'll be out of sight but easily accessible."

Constance nodded as if she approved. It was the first time Maddie had actually seen that she might not be determined to shut down the event.

"There you go! See how useful these committees are?" Rose said. "Now that's settled. Let's finalize the plans and settle on a date so Maddie can get the advertising rolling."

"Not so fast." Constance flipped to another page. "Section twenty-five, article B states liquor cannot be provided unless it is within two hundred feet of a licensed establishment. Now if you put Burt's moonshine display"—her lips curled in distaste at the word—"out in the common area, that will be a violation. And if you plan to serve cocktails on the pier, another violation. I'm afraid you're going to have to adjust your plan."

Constance flipped the notebook shut and sat back in her chair, seeming pleased that she'd thrown a wrench in the works.

"Oh, come on, Connie." Lorna gestured toward the binder. "Those bylaws are ancient. I think we can make an exception."

"That sets a very bad precedent. If we make an exception for this, then someone will want to make an exception for something else, and before you know it, we won't have any laws."

"She has a point," Rose said. "We need to change it legally."

All of Maddie's hopeful expectations were deflated. "Do we have time for that?"

"Could take months, years even," Connie said.

Belinda narrowed her eyes. "Isn't there a mechanism to get around a bylaw temporarily?"

Constance shook her head. "Not that I know of."

Rose sighed. "Maybe we need to rethink some of this. Burt will be disappointed about his moonshine display, and the party is the thing setting the event apart."

Constance stood, clutching her binder. "You're stuck between a rock and a hard place. Without the party, you violate one bylaw, and with it you violate another. I don't know what the solution is, but it seems like you have your work cut out for you if you still want to have this event."

CHAPTER FIFTEEN

The meeting had taken the wind out of Maddie's sails, and she wasn't in the mood for work when she got back to the cottage. Dex gave a cheery hello, and she half waved, trying not to show her disappointment.

Not in the mood to work, she grabbed a beer from the fridge and was hunting in the drawer for a bottle opener when Dex came in to wash out his paintbrushes.

"The meeting didn't go well?" Dex looked truly concerned.

"Not really. They loved my idea, but Constance Harbinger threw up some roadblocks." Maddie told him about the problems Constance had presented.

"Seriously? She's going to nitpick about that?" Dex reached over her and plucked the bottle opener out of the drawer and handed it to her.

"Yeah, but we can't just ignore the bylaws because that would set a precedent, and someone might use that legally to do things in town that no one wants." Maddie flipped the top off her bottle and held it toward him. "Want one?"

He smiled. "Sure."

"I was just going to take a walk down the beach and think things through. You want to join me?" Why in the world did she ask him that? Just two weeks ago, she couldn't stand Dex. Now, he was becoming a friend. Or more. No, just a friend. He couldn't be more, and she didn't want him to. "I'll show you my special spot where I sit sometimes to think things over."

For a second he looked uncertain, and Maddie was afraid she'd overstepped. Hopefully he didn't think she was propositioning him or anything. But then a lazy smile spread on his face. "Of course. Looks like you could use a sounding board."

As soon as Maddie stepped barefoot into the warm sand, she started to feel better. The soothing sounds of the waves, the sunshine, the salt air worked their magic... and the beer didn't hurt either.

They strolled along the water's edge in the wet sand. Dex described how he'd almost finished the exterior, and that the cottage was actually in pretty good shape. That was good news at least.

"I just don't understand Constance. Why is she so angry?" Maddie asked.

Dex's expression turned sympathetic. "I guess she's had it rough. Her husband killed someone drunk driving, and I think she feels guilty even though it had nothing to do with her. Gram said she used to be big into helping in town, but now she's sort of a recluse."

Maddie felt bad. "Oh, maybe I should be kinder to her. Belinda did seem to think there could be a way around it, a temporary exception they could invoke."

"Maybe my grandmother can help with her. She has a way of making people see things differently."

"Do you think so? That would be great." Rose was a fixer, a person who brought others together, a person who got things done. If anyone could help change Constance Harbinger's bad attitude, it was Rose. "Your grandmother is great. She's been very kind to me since I moved to town."

"That's typical Gram. She's really been a big influence my life," Dex said.

"My grandmother was like that too." Maddie inhaled a deep breath of salt air while memories of her grandmother swirled in her head, bringing a nostalgic bittersweet smile to her face. Gram hadn't been gone for very long, and she still missed her.

They'd come to an outcropping of rocks on the beach. Maddie had discovered the jetty on one of her walks. She'd already spent hours exploring the cracks and crevices between the rocks and the puddles left on top for snails, crabs, and starfish. There was a rock that was smooth enough to sit on with a taller rock behind it as a backrest, and she'd taken to thinking of that as "her spot."

The best part was the dramatic view. It looked out over the vast expanse of ocean, but to the right the coastline jutted out, and you could see a tall white lighthouse with a thick red stripe on the middle in the distance.

"I love this place because it's far enough from any of the other houses and public beaches that no one comes here."

Dex grinned. "It's great. I promise not to tell anyone."

"Thanks."

She gestured toward the rock, and they both sat, sipping their beer in silence. Maddie felt a bond of friendship beginning to form.

"Our grandmothers were good friends, weren't they?" Maddie asked. Rose had told her as much, but she knew that Rose, Leena, and Pearl had grown up in Shell Cove, and her grandmother, Rena, had moved here later in life when she bought the Beachcomber Motel.

"Yep. The four of them were really close."

"I can't imagine what they got up to when they were a few decades younger." Maddie laughed

"They were a hoot! They used to hang out at the piano bar in town. Spent most of their nights singing."

Dex chuckled at the memories. "And, of course, they were always organizing things, picnics, meetings. Food was usually involved."

"Their signature dishes." Maddie cringed at the thought of the pretzels she brought to the town meeting. "I'm not as good at that as my grandmother was."

Dex laughed. "Don't worry. One can't be good at everything."

Dex's kind words warmed her.

"Sounds like you and Rose have a special bond," Maddie said.

"We sure do." Dex gazed out at the ocean, his expression pensive.

Maddie's feelings toward him softened. He was nothing like she'd first thought. He wasn't some nonthinking guy who stampeded through life leaving a mess in his wake without caring. Sure, he wasn't as organized as she was, and maybe he didn't think ahead and agonize over every future possibility like she did, but did those things really matter? He was a kind, caring person. His feelings ran deep, and they were in the right place—family and the community of Shell Cove.

She was seeing him with different eyes now.

He turned his gaze from the ocean, and the expression on his face made her think that maybe he was seeing her with different eyes too.

She found herself leaning in toward him, almost as

if a magical force was pushing her. He leaned in, too, his lips slightly parted. His emerald eyes had an intensity to them, and she thought she saw a spark of…

She jerked back.

Had they almost kissed? There was no way she could kiss him! He had a girlfriend.

His eyes widened as if he were just as startled as she was.

He stood and held his beer up. "Beer's gone. Guess we should head back."

Maddie hopped up, happy to oblige.

As they walked back, they fell into easy conversation, but Maddie made sure to keep a safe distance between them.

CHAPTER SIXTEEN

The next day, Dex took Rose to Barnacle Bill's a few towns over for lobster rolls. It was a bimonthly tradition, and something he looked forward to.

The day was hot, the sun bright. They sat out on the deck, watching the boats move in and out of the small cove while gulls circled above hoping for a handout.

The briny smell of the cove water and caw of the gulls spiced the air. Colorful wooden dinghies bobbed in the water at the dock below a row of old, weathered fishing cottages, which were now upscale boutiques. It was about as quaint as New England could be.

The buttered grilled rolls were stuffed full with large chunks of meat coated in mayonnaise. Paprika dusted over the top. They split an order of fries, drank lemon-ade, and enjoyed the easy conversation they always had.

"So what's up with Constance Harbinger?" Dex asked. "Seems like she doesn't want this event to take place. Doesn't she care about Shell Cove?"

Rose pressed her lips together and glanced up at a sailboat that was gliding out of the cove. "Connie has had a hard life. I think she does want Shell Cove to succeed, but she needs to have something she can control. And she can control the bylaws. Not to mention that the whole subject of drinking is a trigger for her after what happened with her husband."

"I can sympathize with that." Dex munched a fry. "So if she just wants to feel in control, then maybe we can help her out by giving her a way to feel in control about the event but still not put so many restrictions on it."

"How?"

"Maddie said that Belinda mentioned there were some temporary exclusions buried somewhere in the town laws. Maybe we could appeal to Constance to figure out what those are and see if we could use them."

"Appeal to her sense of expertise?" Rose mulled it over. "I'm not sure. She might see through us. She's not particularly accommodating, if you haven't noticed."

Dex laughed. "That's for sure."

"It's not really her fault. After the accident, she withdrew. She was downright nasty to anyone who tried to offer her sympathy. She pushed people away. I think she had a lot of guilt even though it wasn't her fault. Then after so many years of pushing people away, everyone eventually stopped trying."

"Well, maybe we can catch her on a good day and persuade her to look into it." Dex was hopeful. He knew Rose would try any angle to make sure the event was a success.

Rose pulled a chunk of lobster claw out of her roll with her fork. "It's worth a try. Let's take a drive past her house on the way back into town."

Constance's house was in a remote area on the edge of Shell Cove, so it was on the way. Dex pulled onto the dirt road at Rose's instruction.

"I didn't realize anyone even lived out here," Dex said as his truck bumped along the ruts.

A weed-filled yard came into view just before an old ranch-style house with peeling paint and a garage with a broken door. A gutter hung down from the roofline.

"Oh, dear. I guess she's let the place get a bit run-down," Rose said.

"Does she have money troubles?" Dex asked.

"Not sure. After her husband died, she might not have had anyone to fix things, and like I said, she's sort of ostracized herself. Maybe she didn't want to hire anyone." Rose sighed. "But it could be money too. I wish I'd known about this. I might have reached out to help."

Dex stopped in front of the house. The driveway was empty, and there was no car in the garage. "Does she have a car?"

"Yes. I guess she isn't home. Sorry, looks like I dragged you out here for nothing."

"No need to apologize. It wasn't for nothing." He turned and drove away, but he wasn't disappointed. He had an idea of what he could do to help Connie come around.

Maddie felt like ripping up all the carefully made drawings and plans sitting on the sectional in front of her. She was so frustrated with this turn of events that even the sounds of the ocean couldn't soothe her. She'd put so much time into this, and now it was ruined. They couldn't have the party on the pier, and they needed the party to attract a good crowd.

She heard Dex's truck pull into the crushed-stone driveway, and a glimmer of hope surfaced. He'd taken Rose to their bimonthly lunch, and hopefully he'd asked her to talk to Constance Harbinger. There had to be a way to bypass the bylaws, at least temporarily.

He was whistling as he came around the corner. A good sign!

"Did Rose talk to Connie?" she asked before even greeting him.

The whistling stopped midnote. "No. We went there, but Connie wasn't home. She said she'd try to talk to her later."

"Oh. Okay."

"What about you? Are you adjusting the plan?" He gestured toward the paperwork.

"Adjusting? No. How can I? It's all planned out to the last detail. Changing it now is impossible."

"I don't think it's impossible. You do have a lot of details, and it will be a lot of work, but it's possible."

What did he know? He was used to working on the fly, never planning anything out. He had no idea how attached one became to the detailed plans.

Maddie frowned down at the paperwork. But he was right. It *could* be changed. Nothing was set in stone, but she was afraid the new iteration wouldn't be as good.

Maddie sighed. "The party is the problem. I don't think people will be happy at a party without cocktails, and if we can't have those down at the pier, it's going to flop."

"Who says the party has to be at the pier? I bet Harley would let you have it at Sharkies, and he has a liquor license."

Maddie scrunched up her face. "But the pier will be so gorgeous lit up at night, and the whole point is to show people how beautiful our town is."

"Maybe there could be another event that focuses on the beach. In the daytime, like sandcastles or surfing."

"Every place has those." Maddie couldn't help the disappointment creeping into her voice. "And then there's Burt's moonshine demonstration. The fan club was really excited about that, but if we have all the tents in the common, then that violates Constance's precious bylaw."

"Maybe we could move the moonshine event into Sharkies. I bet Harley would let him set up in the parking lot. It's out back and not in front of any shops, so it shouldn't be a problem."

"Maybe. I don't know. There's probably a bylaw against setting things up in parking lots. I have put so much time into planning this out, and now it's all a waste."

Dex sat on the sectional beside her. "It's not all a waste. Most of it can still happen the way you planned. I think you need to be a bit more flexible, though. Sometimes you can't get too invested in the vision you have in your head. Sometimes it's not good to plan things out to the smallest detail because it throws you off when things get messed up. And things usually have a way of getting messed up."

"I suppose you're right. I guess I can try to figure something else out for the party." She smiled at Dex. "But in the meantime, I'm still going to hope that Rose can soften Constance up."

"Don't worry. I have an idea that might help bring Connie around to our side."

CHAPTER SEVENTEEN

*G*ina peered into the empty store. It still looked the same, the tables and chairs stacked upon one side, gleaming display cases. She could picture her pies lined up inside.

Word had gotten out that she baked nearly every day now, and people had started to drop by the Beachcomber to see if they could snag a piece of pie. This plus the compliments she'd received at the town meeting had bolstered her confidence, and she was ready to take the next step.

How much would rent cost? She'd have to buy supplies and couldn't count on making a profit right away. She finally had the confidence and motivation to try opening a shop, but now the problem was she didn't have the money, thanks to her cheating husband who'd embezzled it all from their business and then disappeared.

She turned and looked down the street toward the ocean. It was so beautiful here, so much different than Boston. She hadn't wanted to stay here when she'd first come to see the motel she'd inherited, but it had only taken a few weeks for her to fall in love with Shell Cove. But right now, the lack of tourists on the street drove home a painful reality. There might not be enough customers to make her business profitable.

Hopefully Maddie could get things rolling with this new event. Gina wasn't worried that the event was already running up against some roadblocks. She was confident Maddie would figure it out.

She pulled out her phone and thumbed through the contacts, looking for a private investigator. She'd spend the last of her savings to try to find him again. She needed to recover the money he'd stolen from her if she wanted to start her own business.

CHAPTER EIGHTEEN

*R*ose had always taught Dex to be kind to others, and she'd always helped people in need when she could. When Dex saw how dilapidated the Harbinger house was, he'd decided to do the same. Maybe Constance Harbinger would return the kindness by finding a way to ease the restrictions on the event.

He picked up some lumber, gutters, and paint, drove to her house, and started unloading. Rose had told him that she'd be in a meeting at the town hall with Constance for a few hours, so it was the perfect time to start working. He wanted the progress to be well underway before she came back so she couldn't kick him out.

He'd finished hanging the new gutter and was replacing the rotted sill around the garage door when she pulled in.

"Just what do you think you are doing?" she demanded, her expression a mixture of anger and curiosity.

"Hi, Mrs. Harbinger. Do you remember me?" Dex held his hand out for a handshake. "I'm Rose Wisnewski's grandson. I had some extra lumber and was just fixing some things up for you here on the property."

Her suspicion deepened. "Rose's grandson, you say? I was just with Rose at the town hall. She didn't mention anything about this."

"I don't think she knew I was coming out today. I brought her to visit you yesterday, and we saw that you needed some work done. My grandmother said you've been so busy with town business that you probably haven't had time. I had all this extra lumber that was taking up space, so I figured I'd put it to good use." Hopefully he wouldn't get caught in the tiny white lie, but it was for a good reason. And maybe the part about her being too busy with town business would soothe any hurt pride she might have in thinking that Dex and Rose thought she needed charity work.

"Well, you'll have to stop. I don't have the budget to pay for this, and I think it's very presumptuous that you start working without my permission." Constance looked pretty mad.

Dex held his palms up. "No worries. There's no charge for this. Gram said she owed you a favor, and

I'm repaying it. Besides, all these supplies sitting around cost me money. You're actually doing *me* a favor."

More white lies. He was getting in deeper, but somehow he had a feeling Rose would back him up.

Constance frowned. "I did help Rose out a long time ago…"

As she scanned the work he'd done, her pursed lips relaxed. "If it helps you out, I guess I could let you continue."

"It sure does. I'm going to fix this frame so your garage shuts, and then I'll tack the shutter back up and do some scraping and painting. Painting is like therapy to me." Hopefully adding that last part wasn't too over the top.

"All that for free?" She was still skeptical but a bit more friendly.

"Yep. It should only take me the rest of the day."

"Well, okay then." She started toward the front door. "But don't be too loud!"

As Dex went to work, he wondered how he was going to strike up a conversation and persuade her to look into getting around those bylaws. He'd thawed her a bit though, he could tell. He'd think of something.

He needn't have worried. An hour later, she came out with a glass of lemonade.

"It's hot out, and I don't want you collapsing and then suing me."

Her voice was gruff, but Dex appreciated the

gesture, and she even smiled, indicating that she was all bark and no bite.

"Thanks." Now was the perfect time to try to sweet-talk her. "I appreciate it, and I'm glad you're getting some of this fixed."

"I forget what Rose owes me for, but she didn't have to send you out." Her eyes clouded. "Been a long time since anyone did anything neighborly for me."

Dex saw his opening. "Really? Shell Cove is very neighborly. We take care of each other. Maybe you just haven't been open to it." He paused, letting it sink in. "But it might not be that way for long. If we can't attract tourists, then folks might start to leave. Those that are left will keep to themselves. That's why the town event and the Gatsby party are so important."

Constance thought about that, her face a mix of emotions. "I certainly don't want that. But the rules are the rules."

"Have you looked into the special exemptions that Belinda mentioned?" Dex asked. "Surely you could find a way to get around the laws. You know them better than anyone. If there's a loophole, you can find it."

Constance looked pleased, as if she didn't get complimented a lot for her skills. She glanced at the work he'd done on the garage, her expression softening. "Well, I suppose there is one thing I could look into. It might take a while, and I can't make any promises."

CHAPTER NINETEEN

"I'm still forging ahead with the plans just in case we find a way to do the party on the pier. Harley said he'd be happy to host it, but that won't be ideal," Maddie said to her cousins. They were seated on the sectional on Maddie's deck with coffees Jules and Gina had brought from Ocean Brew along with a strawberry pie. "I'm leaning toward still having it there but with no cocktails."

"That will still be fun." Maddie knew Jules was just saying that to be nice, but she appreciated the support.

"Let's talk about the costumes." Gina had the glossy color flyer from the costume shop. "I think you'd look great in one of these beaded ones."

Gina pointed to a gold dress that was loaded with layers of beaded fringe. "That thing looks heavy. I like the red one with the big feather headband." Maddie turned the brochure so they could see the dress. It was a plain sheath but had a beaded headband with a giant feather sticking out of the top.

"Red is a good color for you. I definitely think you should go for that." Jules flipped through the pages. "I love this black-and-silver one."

"I'm going for the turquoise," Gina said.

"Glad we have that settled." Maddie leaned back and picked up her slice of pie. "Now I just need to fit two months of work into one week."

"If you need help, we're available. Not much going on at the motel," Jules said.

"Some of the ads are going into the paper tomorrow, so hopefully you'll get some reservations. I'm holding off on mentioning the Gatsby party, though, until we know the details. Dex said Rose might be able to talk to Constance Harbinger, and I'm still holding out hope that we can figure out a way to lift the town restrictions at least for one night."

"Let's hope," Jules said.

"But if not, the event will still be fun, and it will bring in tourists. The Marco Rosone fan club is excited to come no matter what," Maddie said.

"They're probably just excited about Burt's moonshine demonstration," Gina joked.

Maddie laughed. "That should be interesting, and Harley said he could set something up for him at

Sharkies, so that's a go. Now we just need to see if Rose can work some magic on relaxing those bylaws."

LORELEI DID NOT SEEM THE LEAST BIT IMPRESSED THAT Dex had helped Constance out in an attempt to get her to find a way to ease off on the restrictive bylaws.

She glared at him from her position near the windows in the small living room of his apartment. She had her arms folded over her chest, her expression fixed in a scowl that was becoming all too familiar lately.

"So, you wasted a whole day and a bunch of supplies on some woman who is mean to everyone?" Lorelei looked genuinely confused as to why anyone would do that. "That's not very good business sense."

"It's helping the community, and the community is good business."

"What do you care about a community that you won't even be living in?" she asked. "I mean you *are* still moving in with me in Portland, aren't you?"

Dex paused. Had he actually agreed to move in with her? As far as he could remember, he'd only vaguely nodded his head or said something noncommittal when it came up in conversation. It had always seemed like something that would happen way in the future, and now he was afraid he hadn't put enough thought into it.

Now she was getting that pouty, disappointed look that always made him feel like a jerk. He'd do anything to turn that look into a smile, so he said, "Of course I am. It's just that I have deep ties here, and well, I was thinking maybe I could still keep my place here too."

Lorelei made a face. "Why would you do that?"

Good question. "I'd still want to come back and visit my grandmother and my friends."

Speaking of friends, who would he hang out with in Portland? He loved spending time with Nick and Harley at Sharkies. Would his lifelong friendship with them fade away until they eventually only saw each other a few times a year? And what about Gram? Would he be able to spend as much time with her?

"You can stay at your grandmother's when you come back. I'm sure she'd love to have you. We can't afford two places." Lorelei cocked her head and studied his face. "What's this really about? You don't want to move in with me?"

"No, it's not that." He did want to move in with her. That had pretty much been the plan in his head for over a decade. But in his head, he hadn't considered that meant moving *away* from Shell Cove. Truth be told, he hadn't thought much about what moving in with Lorelei did entail. It had always seemed so far away. He just needed time to get used to the idea.

"Well, if you move to Portland, you're going to be spending a lot more time there. You'll make new friends, and you'll love it there. There's a ton of great restaurants, and you'll still be near the ocean." She hooked her arm through his, and the fact that she seemed happier made him happier. He hated to disappoint her. "You just need to get out of your comfort zone. Once you do, you'll be glad you did."

She was right, of course. He just didn't want to bail on Shell Cove. He wanted to make sure the town had the best chance of growing, and if he could help with that, he wasn't going to let them down. But maybe he *was* spending too much time on it. Time to start focusing more on moving on with the future and less on Shell Cove.

"You're right. Let's plan a fun two days in Portland, and you can show me some of your favorite places." Dex realized he hadn't spent much time there. It was time to give the city a chance.

"Now you're talking." She kissed him on the cheek, and her bright smile was worth the brick of worry weighing down his heart. A worry that made him afraid that this time going with the flow might not be the right thing to do.

CHAPTER TWENTY

*M*addie had placed advertisements for the event in every local paper and even some of the major ones. She'd made up flyers and driven them to the chambers of commerce in other towns. She'd posted all over social media. She'd arranged for tents, porta potties, and even more trash barrels to temporarily place in town.

But the one thing that hadn't happened was no one had figured out how to get around the bylaws to have the party on the pier. Sure, they could have it at Sharkies, but the pub only had capacity for eighty, and Maddie was expecting a lot more than that. If they stuck with the pier, then they could have more people. But what fun was a dry party, especially when it was in the middle of an event for an infamous bootlegger?

People were excited about the party too. Jules had

gotten several reservations for that weekend, and they had mentioned the Great Gatsby party specifically and wanted to know where they could rent costumes.

It was a good sign that people were booking rooms, and Maddie was optimistic about the event bringing people to town. So when Rose called to tell her Constance had called an emergency meeting of the planning committee, she couldn't help but feel a sense of impending doom.

The rest of the committee might have felt the same, if the looks on their faces as Maddie entered the small room in the town hall were any indication. She took a seat next to Rose. Where was Constance?

"Maybe you could update us on the progress while we wait for Connie," Rose said.

Maddie was in the middle of the update when the door opened and Constance entered. She looked different than normal. Usually, she dressed in frumpy outdated clothing. Today she wore a clean white blouse and sharp linen capris. It might not have been the clothing that made her look so different, though. It might have been the fact that she was smiling.

"I'm so sorry I'm late." Constance pulled out a chair and sat, arranging a stack of papers in front of her. "The printer down the hall wasn't cooperating."

"It's fine," Rose said. "Maddie just updated us on the project."

"Oh?"Constance looked at Maddie. "Things are going well?"

Was she asking because she was hoping to put another wrench in the works? "As well as can be, considering the restrictions."

"I see. Well then, I think I have good news. I might have found a way to loosen the restrictions for the event." Constance started handing out stapled packets from her pile.

Maddie was speechless. She glanced at Rose. Rose appeared surprised too.

"This is great. I knew there was a workaround." Belinda pointed to a paragraph in the middle of the first page. "See here, there is a town ordinance waiver that we can put in place for special events."

Maddie leafed through the papers. They were copies of various pages from the town laws and then a written-up recommendation at the end to enact the temporary workaround.

"You mean we can have the party on the pier now, and Burt can set up his demonstration on the common?" Maddie asked.

"I believe so. Unless anyone sees something wrong in the packet?" Constance looked around the table, but no one raised an objection.

"It looks in order to me," Belinda said.

"Me too," Lorna agreed.

"Well, I'm not about to try to find fault in it." Alice

closed her packet and folded her hands on top of it. "So do we have to do something official to get this enacted?"

"I believe there are enough of the town officers here for a quorum, so all we have to do is vote," Constance said.

"Well, in that case." Rose stood. "Everyone in favor of enacting the temporary orders, say 'aye.'"

Maddie half expected Constance to throw another curveball at them at the last minute, but she loudly said, "Aye." As did everyone else. It was unanimous!

"Thank you so much, Connie, for doing this work. I'm thrilled you saw your way to helping our town." Rose beamed at Connie, who looked uncomfortable, as if she wasn't used to helping out.

"Well, it's only fair. In Shell Cove, we help each other out, and someone recently helped me. That reminded me of how nice it is to be a giving member of the community. As you know, I've been a little withdrawn lately, but now I want to get involved, and this is my way of helping the town."

"That's wonderful news!" Rose said.

"It is." Belinda patted Constance on the hand, and the woman actually blushed.

Maddie walked beside Rose on the way out. "I guess whatever you said to Connie must have really made her see things differently."

"That's the funny thing. I never did get a chance to talk to her."

"Really? Then what was all that about someone helping her?"

Rose smiled. "I have no idea, but let's not question it. The important thing is we can have the event the way we wanted it."

CHAPTER TWENTY-ONE

*T*he party was on! Maddie wasted no time in arranging things for it to happen at the pier. Caterers, a tent for outside, strings of white lights to wind around the tent and tables. Dex built a solid platform for dancing. It was going to be amazing, mingling and dancing under the stars with the ocean below.

The Beachcomber was overflowing with reservations, and the costume store was racking up orders. Deena and Chuck were making extra orders of the whisky fudge and freezing it in anticipation of the demand.

It had been an exhausting week, but Maddie didn't mind. She had the feeling that after this event, people were going to go back home and talk about Shell Cove to their families and neighbors, and that was exactly what she wanted.

Dex had gone overboard helping her, and she'd gotten used to his company. It turned out they had a lot in common, and his way of flying by the seat of his pants did have some merits. She'd gotten him to admit that her way of planning had merits, too, and she'd even caught him making a timeline of sorts for the progress on her cottage.

The cottage was only coming along slowly, though, since he was spending most of his time on the event. Maddie didn't mind. The town was more important, and her cottage would still be there after.

She was on the pier with the tent company, trying to figure out the exact placement, when Lorelei strolled up.

"Dex told me Constance let go of her witchy ways, and you can have the party here. It's a good spot," Lorelei said.

"Yeah, that was nice of her." Maddie felt awkward, but maybe this was Lorelei's attempt to make friends, seeing as Maddie had become such good friends with Dex. But there was something off about her, as if some other purpose was simmering under the surface.

"Well, she should be nice after what Dex did for her."

Maddie was confused. "What did he do for her?"

Lorelei's left brow rose. "He didn't tell you? Her property was a mess. She hadn't been taking care of it, so he went over and fixed things up for her."

Rose had said she didn't know who was responsible for Constance's change of heart. Had it been Dex? She smiled, thinking of his kindness in fixing up Constance's house and doing it so the town could have the party on the pier just like she wanted.

"That was nice of him. He's a nice guy," Maddie said.

"He is. I'm surprised he didn't tell you, seeing as you spend so much time together."

Did she detect a tinge of jealousy in her voice? "We're not that close. We have worked on a lot of the things for the event together, but we're busy working. It's not like we hang out." Except for that time on the beach where she'd felt that tug of a connection.

Lorelei bent over to inspect the pot of colorful flowers in front of the old donut shop. Lorna had put it there for the baking contest and had kept it up. Lorelei plucked a bright-yellow marigold off its stem. "Then I guess it won't affect you too much that he's leaving."

"Leaving?" Dex was leaving? What did she mean? Were they going on vacation? He hadn't mentioned it, but then again, it wasn't like they were besties.

Lorelei sniffed the flower, glancing up at Maddie from under her dark lashes. "He's moving to Portland to be with me, of course. We've planned it for ages. In fact, we're going to pick out a place this weekend."

"Oh, of course. I knew that, just didn't realize it was going to be so soon."

"Yep. So I hope you won't be needing him to do too much more here in Shell Cove."

"Of course not. I can handle the rest of this." Hopefully he was sticking around long enough to finish her cottage.

"Great. Then I'll let you get back to work." Lorelei tossed the flower over the side of the railing and sauntered off, her high heels clacking on the wood of the pier.

A cloud of disappointment dampened Maddie's excitement. But why? She knew Lorelei lived in Portland, and it made sense that Dex would move in with her. Maybe it was because, even though they'd been working closely and she'd thought they'd become friends, he hadn't mentioned anything about moving soon. That stung. Apparently, they weren't as close as she'd assumed. Better to keep things on a professional level from here on out.

CHAPTER TWENTY-TWO

"*Y*ou're serious about moving out of Shell Cove?"

Dex could see the doubt in Nick's eyes. He glanced around the empty bar at Sharkies, where they had met for a late-afternoon beer. "Yeah. I think."

"You think? That's a pretty big move." Nick took a sip from his frosty beer mug.

"I know." What else could he say? He still hadn't quite come to terms with it himself.

"Well, I'll miss you man. So, you're leaving this weekend?"

"What?" Dex jerked his head up, startled. "Oh, no, we're just going there for the weekend. I'll be back Monday."

"Oh, I heard something about you picking out a place."

"Where did you hear that?" Dex was certain Lorelei never mentioned anything about that. He'd assumed they'd move into her place.

"Jules. I think she heard from Maddie. I might have gotten mixed up though."

Maddie had been talking about him moving? He hadn't mentioned it to her. Not because he didn't want to. It was because she'd been acting a little strange, and he couldn't quite put his finger on it. He'd thought they were becoming close, like they could talk about anything, but the past few days she'd seemed distant. Not cold-shoulder distant, but just not as... intimate. Intimate? That wasn't exactly the right word, or was it?

"Are you sure about this? I mean, Rose is here, and your friends are here." Nick pointed to himself.

Dex laughed, but Nick's words gave him pause. *Was* he sure? The thought of not waking up every day in Shell Cove made his stomach hurt, but maybe that was more about what he was used to. Like Lorelei had said, getting out of your comfort zone felt uncomfortable.

"Lorelei is pretty set on it," Dex said.

"And you're set on Lorelei." Nick said it as a statement, but Dex knew his friend well enough to sense it was a question.

"Well, yeah. I mean we've been dating for a long time." Dex looked at Nick. He'd changed since meeting Jules. He was always smiling, and Dex could always tell when Jules walked into the room by the way Nick lit up. Their longing glances and the way they always touched each other bordered on sickening. He didn't have that with Lorelei, at least not anymore. But that was to be expected after so many years, wasn't it?

But then Dex thought about his grandmother and grandfather. They'd still shared those looks and touches. His grandfather had lit up when Rose walked into the room up until the day he'd died. And they'd been together a lot longer than Dex and Lorelei.

"It's about time you settled down, and if Lorelei is the one, then you need to move." Nick's tone was warm, but Dex knew he didn't really care for Lorelei. "I'm glad you'll be around for a while anyway. You guys are coming to the big party, right? It's all Jules has been talking about."

"I think so." Naturally Dex wanted to go, but Lorelei hadn't seemed so keen on it when he'd asked her.

"Good. I won't feel as silly in a dumb costume with you in one too." Nick made a face. "But I have to wear one. I don't want to disappoint Jules, and Maddie has worked so hard on this."

"Of course. Costumes it is." Dex could understand Nick not wanting to disappoint Jules. He hated it when Lorelei was disappointed. But he had a feeling that was for a different reason entirely. Lorelei acted like a spoiled princess and made Dex miserable when she was disappointed. Nick didn't want to disappoint Jules because he was disappointed when she was. There was a big difference.

Suddenly Dex was starting to question everything. Was he making a huge mistake?

CHAPTER TWENTY-THREE

*G*ina had spent the last week poring over her pie recipes, getting ingredients, and planning for the event. The Beachcomber had a tent in the merchant section, and she wanted to offer free pieces of pie. Jules had been busy getting pamphlets made and putting together a binder with pictures of the motel, the rooms, the lobby, and of course, the porch overlooking the ocean.

She'd spent the last of the proceeds from the convertible she'd traded for something less expensive when she came to Shell Cove on the retainer for the private investigator. She didn't have any savings—Hugh had taken all of it—but the motel was fully booked for the next week, and even more reservations were coming in for future weeks, so she'd have money soon. The advertising for the event was working and bringing attention to the town, and people seemed eager to vacation here even after the event was over.

She was feeling more hopeful about Shell Cove, but that also created a sense of urgency for renting the old bakery. She'd gone as far as to inquire about it and had worked a deal to get reduced rent for fixing it up, not that it needed much work. She got the impression that the owner was just happy at the prospect of receiving rent since the store had been empty for five years. She hadn't agreed just yet, though.

The offer might not last long. If tourists started to come back, merchants might be rushing to open stores. Still, she wasn't going to make a decision until she found out if she could locate Hugh. She wanted to know how much money she had to work with.

"I can't believe how many people are buzzing around town already." Maddie breezed in through the side door to the kitchen with a tray of coffees from Ocean Brew. "I had to wait in line for these!"

"It's a good sign," Jules said. "The motel is fully booked for two weeks, and we got a few reservations for next month too."

Maddie handed out the coffees, a hopeful look of excitement on her face. "Let's hope this is the thing that keeps people thinking about and coming back to Shell Cove."

"I'll drink to that." Gina held out her Styrofoam cup, and they clinked rims.

"So what's left to do? Can we help with anything?" Jules asked.

Maddie shook her head. "Everything is going smooth as butter. The tents are being set up right now, and I'm going to go down after to double-check on that. The caterer is going to start prep in the old donut shop on the pier at noon for the party tomorrow. There's nothing left to do but enjoy."

"Well, in that case, I say we get our costumes today and try them on here tomorrow night before the party. Then we can all go to it together," Jules said.

"And Nick?" Gina teased.

"I'm meeting him there, nosy," Jules said. "I wanted to hang out with my favorite cousins a little first."

Gina smiled. It felt good to be a favorite cousin, though that hadn't always been the case. The three of them had come far in their relationship since inheriting the motel, and that was worth moving out here, even if her dreams of a pie shop never came true.

CHAPTER TWENTY-FOUR

*D*ex sat on the front steps of Starfish Cottage and unwrapped the sandwich Rose had brought him. Tuna fish, just like she used to make when he was a kid. This did not bode well. She only reverted to that when she had something important to talk about.

She sat down beside him, reached into the wicker picnic basket she'd used to transport the sandwich, and pulled out a bag of chips, which she opened and tilted in his direction. "The cottage is coming along nicely. Where's Maddie? I brought an extra sandwich."

He grabbed a handful of chips and put them on the red-checked paper plate Rose had provided. "She's over at the Beachcomber visiting with her cousins."

Dex wondered why he hadn't seen much of Maddie lately. It wasn't exactly like she was avoiding him. She'd been pleasant when their paths had crossed. They'd both been so busy that they hadn't had much time to chat. Dex missed that. He felt like there was a little hole in his life now that he wasn't spending as much time with her.

With most of the work done now for the event, he'd been focusing on the cottage. He didn't know when he was going to be moving, but he wanted to finish up here before he did. He still needed to address the feeling of doom whenever he thought about moving.

"That's nice. I ran into her yesterday, and she's excited about the party." Rose tore a corner off her own sandwich and sighed. "I can't believe you're not going to the party. You worked so hard on everything, seems a shame for you to miss it."

"I promised Lorelei I'd go to Portland so she could show me her favorite places, and that's when she wants to go. I guess those are going to be my favorite places now too." Dex could feel the disappointment radiating from his grandmother and could barely look at her. Nick was going to be disappointed too. When he'd promised Lorelei, he hadn't realized she meant to go on the weekend of the event, but he hadn't been able to persuade her to change it. "I'm not much for dressing up, anyway."

"It's funny. I would think Lorelei would want to be here for the event and the party too. She's from Shell Cove. You'd think she'd want the town to be successful."

"I guess she's just not as attached to the town as we are." Dex took another bite of the tuna, but the usually delicious sandwich now tasted like sawdust.

"That's too bad." Rose popped the last of her sandwich into her mouth and brushed the crumbs from her fingers. "But I guess when you truly love someone, it doesn't matter where you live. As long as you and Lorelei are together, it won't be a huge sacrifice for you to not live in Shell Cove."

Dex swallowed hard. Doubts roared in his head. He'd never questioned his love for Lorelei, but when Rose put it that way... "You moved to live with Gramps here in Shell Cove. Did you ever regret it?"

Rose smiled. "Not a minute. I would have lived anywhere with him, but the town is beautiful, and the people, too, so that was a bonus."

"How did you know it was the right thing?"

Rose smiled, a faraway look in her eye. "Well, you just know. Nothing is more important than being with that person, and every time you see them your heart is filled with joy." She turned to him, her expression now quizzical. "You know what I mean, of course."

Dex gave her a half smile. He couldn't exactly say that he did. He felt happy when he saw Lorelei... well, most of the time. But joy? And sometimes when she was in Portland and he was here, well, those were some of his best days.

"Of course, you have that with Lorelei or you

wouldn't be moving so far away from everything else you love. You're much too smart to just float along a path you don't really desire just because it's something you've had in your head for a long time." Rose patted his knee. "I just hope you remember to come back and visit your old grandmother."

Dex hugged her. "Of course I will, Gram."

"Okay then." Rose jumped up and started putting everything away in the picnic basket. "I hope our little talk has been enlightening."

"As always." Dex helped her pack up the plates, napkins, and chips. But his mind wasn't on the task.

His brain was whirling on Rose's words—not to float along a path just because you'd had it in your head for a long time. Was that what he had done? Settled on something in his head instead of taking the time to think about what he really wanted? And why did it seem like his grandmother's words had a lot more weight than the casual way in which they'd been said? Rose always did know what was best for him.

CHAPTER TWENTY-FIVE

*R*ose swirled a packet of sugar into her steaming coffee and smiled up at Aggie Fletcher, who was seated across the café table just outside Ocean Brew. Pearl, Rose, and Leena had bumped into Aggie around town a few times and decided to ask her for coffee. She had accepted enthusiastically and had proven to be good company, smart and vivacious. Today she was as chipper as ever, her red hair made even brighter in the summer sun. Her face was dotted with freckles, and her nose was red from too much time on the beach.

Rose had more to smile about than just a new friend. It was a crisp summer morning, the birds were singing, and the tents for the event were set up in the common and buzzing with activity. More tourists milled about in front of the stores on the street, holding colorful bags loaded with purchases. Maddie's event was already working its magic.

"The town is awakening. I can feel it. This is the very thing we needed." Pearl pinched a crumb off the top of her bran muffin. They'd each ordered muffins—Pearl's was bran, Leena's was blueberry, Rose opted for lemon poppy seed, and Aggie got the chocolate muffin with chocolate chips.

"What made Connie change her mind?" Leena asked.

Rose had driven past Connie's house and seen the repairs. She knew Dex had done them, but he was too humble to brag, and when she mentioned it, he made light of it saying he'd noticed how run-down it was the day he had brought Rose out and just happened to have the exact lumber and supplies on hand to fix it up. Only someone who really loved the town would go to those lengths. Dex just couldn't move away. He would be miserable.

"I think she just remembered how we help each other and how she loved the town and figured out how to make it work," Rose said. Dex wouldn't want her telling everyone what he'd done.

"I saw them doing some preliminary setup down at the old donut shop. I guess the tent for the party will go up tomorrow." Aggie's eyes twinkled. "It's very exciting."

"Were you able to talk Henry into wearing a

costume?" Rose was skeptical. Henry never was one to dress up for parties when they were younger, and Rose didn't think he'd be more receptive to it in his old age.

"It took some doing, but I managed. I love dressing up." Aggie waved her arms, letting the sleeves of the rainbow-colored caftan float out like butterfly wings as if to illustrate.

"If you've talked him into that, I must say he must be very sweet on you." Pearl smiled at Aggie warmly.

Aggie blushed. "We do get along well."

"So what are you wearing, Rose?" Pearl asked.

"I'm going with classic black, and I have an outrageous peacock feather hat. What about you?"

"I'm wearing a peach sheath dress, nothing too fancy, but I do have a long strand of pearls that were my mother's, and I'm going to wear those." It was just like Pearl to be understated, and pearls were her signature gem.

"Leena?"

Leena made a face. "I'm not much for fancy dresses. I was thinking about wearing one of the suits."

"A pinstripe suit would look great on you!" Rose, Pearl, and Aggie agreed.

Leena looked pleased at the compliment. "Then that's what I'll wear."

"I'm wearing hot pink with lots of fringe," Aggie said. "Don't worry, it's not too flamboyant."

"We've sort of come to expect flamboyant from you." Leena gestured toward Aggie's flowing sleeves.

Aggie laughed. "I guess so."

"It's good to be known for something," Rose said, lest Aggie think they disapproved. Quite the contrary, the ladies had agreed Aggie was a lot of fun.

Pearl turned to Rose. "Dex worked really hard on this event. I saw him down here a few times measuring things and building supports for the tents in the common."

Leena snorted. "Yeah, Burt's moonshine tent needed a lot of work. He had to build a special platform"

Aggie laughed. "Ugh... did you try any of that? That stuff will rot your stomach out."

"Sure will, but the tourists seem to like it," Leena said.

"Those Marco Rosone enthusiasts ate it up... or should I say *drank* it up," Pearl said. "I heard a lot of them remarking on how quaint the town was and how they wanted to come back on vacation."

"I still can't believe that Dex wants to move away after putting all this work in." Leena frowned at Rose.

"Don't be too sure about that," Rose said. "He's been asking some serious questions, and I have a feeling that he's going to see that Shell Cove is exactly where he belongs."

"But what about Lorelei?" Leena asked. "Will she stay here too?"

"I don't think so. I'm pretty sure Dex is starting to see that she might not be the one for him. Why are you asking? Are you worried about your bet?"

Leena laughed. "Maybe. But I know you don't love the idea of Lorelei for a granddaughter-in-law, and you want Dex to stay in town near you, so I'll be happy for you if he stays. Besides, the bet was for Mex—Maddie and Dex—so I could still win because even if he stays in town, there is no indication the two of them will get together."

"I don't know. Have you seen the way those two look at each other?" Pearl asked.

"One can only hope!" Rose had grown fond of Maddie and loved the idea of her getting together with Dex.

"Don't worry, Leena, we still have the Chuck and Deena bet to win. What did you guys call it? Chukeena?" Aggie glanced over at Saltwater Sweets. "Those two have their work cut out for them, and you know how people are when it comes to kids. No matter how old your kids are, you don't want to disappoint them. They might just break up if they can't get the kids to approve."

"True. I hate to see Deena unhappy, though," Leena said. "But I do like to win bets."

"There's another new couple in town we could bet on." Rose jerked her head toward Aggie. "Haggie."

Everyone laughed, including Aggie.

"So what do you say? You want in on that bet?" Pearl asked Aggie.

Aggie shrugged and sipped her coffee. "I think I'd have to disqualify myself because I have insider information, but if I were you, I wouldn't bet against us."

CHAPTER TWENTY-SIX

"We can go to Portland any weekend. This is the only weekend that Shell Cove has a big event." Dex was a bit perplexed and disappointed at Lorelei's vehement protest to staying in town.

"But you promised." She pouted.

"Right. But I didn't think it through, so I didn't realize that you wanted to go on the weekend of the big event. Don't you want to go to the Gatsby party? It will be fun. All our friends from town will be there."

"I don't care about a silly party."

Now she was acting like a spoiled brat. Where was the sweet, easygoing Lorelei that he'd fallen for?

"You used to like costume parties," Dex pointed out.

"I still do. But I don't really have any friends here in town anymore. Everyone in town is so... stuck in their ways. None of our friends that have stayed here are leveling up in their careers like I am."

"Leveling up?" Dex was happy doing carpentry. He loved creating things, and the job was different every day. Plus it had the added benefit of helping people. Suddenly he was wary of what Lorelei's version of leveling up would be for him. Would she try to pressure him into some other sort of job?

"Yeah, you know, career growth and all. There are no opportunities here. You need to be in the city if you want to make something of yourself."

"Really? I already *am* something."

She gave him a sad, pitying look. "Of course, you are. But if you got a job at one of the big companies as a maintenance guy, you'd have a 401k and benefits. Or if you signed on to one of the commercial crews, you'd get salary and paid vacations."

"I don't want to work for someone else. I like working for myself." Working on a commercial building crew or as a maintenance guy was the last thing Dex wanted to do. But judging by the look on Lorelei's face, that was exactly the plan she had for him. Suddenly Dex realized that maybe the vision he'd had in his head all these years and the vision Lorelei had had were two different things. He didn't necessarily like her version.

"We can talk about that when you move there." She suddenly turned cheerful. "This weekend we can check out some of the bigger apartments. Mine is too small."

Dex was seeing a different side of Lorelei. All this time, he'd held onto the girl he'd known since high school, but this woman was not that girl. And suddenly he realized that she was not his future.

"I'm not going to Portland this weekend." The words came out slow as if he was measuring each one. Which he was.

Her eyes turned cloudy, and Dex braced for one of her tantrums. "Fine! If you want to go to the party that bad, we can stay here, but I have nothing to wear and all the good costumes are probably taken."

"It's not just this weekend. I'm not *moving* there." Dex hadn't actually known he was going to say that, but as soon as the words had left his mouth, he knew they were the right ones.

"What? Are you joking?"

"No, I'm sorry. It's just that I love Shell Cove, and I don't want to move. I don't want a new job. I don't want to leave my friends."

Lorelei was furious. "Is this about that cottage girl?"

"Maddie?"

"Yeah, whatever her name is. I've seen you guys looking at each other."

"We kind of have to look at each other. We were working together." Dex had no idea what she was talking about. Had Maddie been looking at him? Surprisingly, the thought made his heart do a little skip.

"Well, I doubt she's going to be waiting for you to

take her to the party. I'm sure she'll find someone else. Especially after I told her that you're moving away."

Dex frowned. "Wait. You told her that? When did you talk to her?"

"The other day." Now Lorelei looked guilty. If Dex had to guess, maybe she'd said a lot more than that he was moving. And that explained why Maddie had been acting a bit standoffish.

It also drove home the fact that Dex was making the right decision. He didn't know who this Lorelei standing in front of him was, but it wasn't the girl he'd fallen in love with. And it certainly wasn't the girl he wanted to spend the rest of his life with.

CHAPTER TWENTY-SEVEN

*M*addie walked around the cottage, surveying the work Dex had done during the day while she'd been downtown working on the event.

She'd stayed at the event until almost seven, so she wasn't surprised to discover Dex had left by the time she got home. It was Friday, so he was probably on his way to Portland with Lorelei.

The first day of the event had gone off without a hitch, and both the merchants in the tents and the shops had reported robust sales. Sully's was almost out of ice cream, and that was a good sign. Maddie didn't need signs, though. She could tell by the swell of tourists that the event was a success.

The president of the Marco Rosone fan club had been pleased and even said this was better than the one they usually had in New York. He wanted to have one in Shell Cove every year. Even better, she'd overheard several tourists saying that they wanted to come back for a relaxing vacation. They'd loved Burt's moonshine exhibit, and Maddie had to admit the old guy really gave a good show.

Dex had finished most of the work on the walls in the living room and dining room, and the place was starting to shape up. The cabinets still needed work—she'd been busy with the event and hadn't had a chance to do more sanding—but they were useable, and that was a project she could plug away at when things settled down.

She stepped over one of the tools strewn about the floor of the living room without a thought. Funny thing, she was just getting used to Dex's disorganized mess, and now he'd be gone. She brushed away feelings of sadness. Dex was going to live with his true love, and she was happy for him. It was funny. At first she would have been unaffected at his leaving town—maybe even glad—but now she felt a hole in her life.

She grabbed a glass of wine and opened the door to the outdoor deck. The tide was coming in, and she could hear the roar of the waves crashing on the beach. She inhaled deeply, tasting the salty, humid air. The full moon sparked off the crests of the waves. She was exhausted from the day, but a sense of satisfaction filled her. She had a strong feeling that Shell Cove, the Beach-comber, and Starfish Cottage were going to be okay.

She settled into the sectional and sipped her wine. She would call it an early night. With the Gatsby party to set up for tomorrow and then the party itself tomorrow night, it was going to be a long day.

CHAPTER TWENTY-EIGHT

Sharkies was more crowded than Dex had ever seen it, but Dex hadn't minded, elbowing his way through the crowd. He and Nick were seated at one of the high-top tables with frosty mugs, and Nick was looking at him in confusion.

"So you broke up with her? Just the other day you were going to move to Portland to move in with her."

"I know. Crazy, right? But I realized that moving to Portland isn't really what I want. And maybe Lorelei isn't the one for me." Dex had agonized over the decision all night but still felt it was the right one.

Nick broke into a big smile. "Finally! I could have told you that, but you're too hardheaded to listen."

Dex laughed. There was nothing better than joking around with your oldest friend, and now that he wasn't moving, he could look forward to much more of that. Another reason he knew he'd made the right decision.

"So you're going to that party on the pier then?" Nick looked hopeful.

"I guess."

"You have to. I don't want to be the only one dressed in one of those old suits."

"Do we really have to dress up?" Dex didn't love the idea.

"According to Jules, I do, and I sure would appreciate the company. It will be fun. At least that's what Jules said." Nick made a face, and Dex knew he didn't think it would be fun at all but was doing it for Jules.

"I suppose I could."

"Great. We can go to the costume store and pick something out. I'm supposed to wear a hat with a silver band. Don't let me forget."

"Why silver?"

"To match with her dress. Jules went into great detail about their dresses. Hers is black and silver, and Maddie's has a giant red feather that sticks up from the headband. Gina's is turquoise."

"Boy, you're really getting into girls' fashions," Dex teased.

Nick shrugged. "Whatever makes her happy. Let's finish these and get to the costume store before they're sold out."

CHAPTER TWENTY-NINE

$\mathcal{M}$addie was exhausted. She'd spent the day running from the tent area to the pier and back again. There had been a problem with Burt's moonshine. The barrel had spilled, and the whole merchant area smelled of whisky. It probably wouldn't be too good for the grass, either. She'd straightened things out there just in time to run down to the pier and get the caterer set up in the old donut shop.

She'd been so busy that she hadn't had a chance to check in with her cousins and see how things had gone in the Beachcomber vendor tent. When she was done with her tasks, she drove straight to the Beachcomber Motel to meet them to get dressed for the party.

"You guys should see the pier! It looks amazing with the twinkle lights in the tent and round high-tops that you can stand and set your drinks on. It's going to be amazing, dancing under the stars tonight."

"How romantic." Jules looked starry-eyed, and Maddie and Gina exchanged disgusted glances. The longer Jules dated Nick, the sappier she got.

"So how did things go in the tent today?" Maddie asked as they took their dresses out of the bags in the lobby. Gina was still set up in the storage room as her living space, and they would change in there in case someone came in.

"Pretty good. Everyone loved Gina's pies." Jules pulled her dress out of the bag and held it up in front of her. It was gorgeous, with a black satin lining and beads of silver in a geometric design. The bottom had at least three inches of silver fringe. Jules jiggled it so the fringe swayed.

"You're going to look great dancing." Gina inspected her own dress. It was a gorgeous shade of turquoise, low waisted with scalloped tiers of fringe on the bottom half.

"I'm going to try mine on." Jules practically skipped to Gina's room.

"So, what kinds of pies did you make? Sorry I didn't get a chance to stop by." Maddie slid the plastic off her dress. The shade of red was gorgeous, and the beaded detail on the sleeves and hem were better than she'd expected, though the dress seemed a little big.

"No worries. I know you were busy." Gina hung

the coat hanger on the arm of a floor lamp and fluffed out the skirt of her dress. "I made three apple, since everyone loves those, and one rhubarb and one peach."

Maddie smiled at the obvious excitement in her cousin's voice. "I bet people gobbled those up."

"They did. They even called their friends over to try a slice."

"You're getting really good at the pies. Have you thought any more about doing it professionally?"

Gina looked away, but not before Maddie saw a sly smile. Gina was thinking about it but wanted to keep it to herself for now. Maddie didn't want to press her.

"Maybe. But right now, the motel needs my help."

Suddenly Maddie felt guilty. "I'm sorry that I haven't been around. I hate leaving all the work to you guys. The three of us are supposed to be a team."

Gina touched her arm. "Don't feel bad. You're doing the most important job of all, bringing people to Shell Cove. And it's working."

"Ta-da!" Jules emerged from Gina's room. She'd put her long dark hair into a roll at the nape of her neck and looked radiant.

"You look amazing!" Gina said.

"Just gorgeous." Maddie smiled as Jules turned this way and that, letting the beaded fringe fly out.

"Come on, you guys need to change so I can see what you look like." Jules glanced at the clock. "We're supposed to meet Rose, Leena, and Pearl in fifteen minutes."

Maddie went into the bathroom next to the kitchen, and Gina into her room. But as soon as Maddie pulled the dress over her head, she knew it was going to take more than a few pins to make it fit. She was practically swimming in it.

She poked her head out of the bathroom. "Uh, guys, I don't think this dress is going to work."

"Why?" Gina had already put her dress on. The turquoise color brought out the green in her eyes. Strings of beads dripped from every inch of it, and it fit her like a glove, unlike Maddie's, which fit her like a tent.

She widened the door and stepped out. "It's a bit too big."

Gina and Jules gaped then tried to arrange their expressions to not look so horrified.

"I'm sure we can do something…" Jules glanced at Gina.

"Yeah, maybe some pins or—"

"Yoo-hoo! Are you girls here?" someone yelled from the lobby.

"In here!" Jules yelled out. "That sounded like Aggie."

Aggie rushed around the corner, holding out a hot-pink dress in front of her. "My dress. It's way too small!"

The dress was simple but stunning with a plain, scooped-neck bodice, cap sleeves, and inches of layered fringe on the bottom.

Jules looked from Aggie to Maddie. "Interesting development. Maddie's is too big. Maybe you guys should swap."

The pink dress fit Maddie perfectly. The red was still a little big on Aggie.

"It's great. I like having room to move around. Henry promised me a night filled with dancing." Aggie swiveled her hips to show off her dance moves.

"Careful, don't break anything," Gina said.

"Don't forget this." Jules placed the headband with the ginormous red feather on Aggie's head.

She glanced in the mirror. "Oh, I love it! Are you girls heading out?"

"In a minute. I think Maddie needs new shoes. Those red ones clash with the pink dress," Jules said. "I have a pair in my room that would be perfect."

CHAPTER THIRTY

*J*ules's hot-pink satin shoes did fit perfectly, although the heels were a bit higher than what Maddie was used to. They took two cars to the party. Nick could give Jules a ride back when she wanted, but Gina and Maddie wanted to go separately. Maddie was exhausted and didn't know if she'd stay long.

The small parking lot near the pier was full, and they had to park a block away, but Maddie couldn't complain. The turnout had exceeded her expectations.

"It looks amazing!" Jules said as they approached the pier. The crowd buzzed with excitement as women in sequined cocktail dresses and men in suits with 1930s-style hats mingled. The tent glowed with warm light from the faux candles on the tables, and the tiny lights strung along the tent poles and edges of the tent canopy gave it a magical feel. It was a cloudless night, and the stars shone bright alongside the crescent moon.

They ran into Deena and Chuck as soon as they stepped on the pier. The couple was holding hands and looked cute with Chuck in a white suit and two-toned wingtips and Deena in a simple sheath dress that looked quite elegant.

"You girls look lovely," Chuck said.

"Thanks so much. You guys look great," Jules answered.

"The party is fabulous." Deena gestured to the crowd on the pier. "I hear most of that is down to you, Maddie."

"Oh no, I had a lot of help."

"Well, you all did a great job." Chuck's smile was genuine and kind. "And we'd like to thank you girls for the discount on rooms over at the Beachcomber. Our children have agreed to come to town."

Chuck glanced at Deena, and the two of them suddenly didn't look so happy.

"We have a plan to help them accept that we are right for each other." Deena hugged Chuck's arm.

"Hopefully it won't backfire," Chuck said wistfully.

"Let's hope. Anyway, we can't have them with us. It would be too awkward, so getting a discount on the rooms was a big help. We want you girls to have a discount on your purchases at Saltwater Sweets to help repay you," Deena said.

"Thank you. That's very kind but not necessary," Gina said.

"It's our pleasure. Now if you'll excuse us, we need to grab some champagne."

The happy couple walked away, and the three cousins scanned the crowd. Maddie figured Jules was looking for Nick. Thoughts of Dex bubbled up. Of course, he wouldn't be with Nick tonight. He was with Lorelei, and why in the world was she thinking of him anyway?

"Oh, look, there's the welcome wagon ladies." Jules pointed into the crowd, and Maddie squinted to see the three senior citizens in a group of people laughing. Pearl and Rose looked elegant, Pearl with a simple sheath dress and pearls dangling to her waist, Rose in black with a colorful peacock feather artfully placed on her head. Both women had matching beaded purses dangling from their wrists. Leena looked the best though. She wore a pinstripe suit and off-white fedora.

Pearl was gesturing with a long cigarette holder she held in her right hand. Maddie was glad to see there wasn't actually a cigarette in it.

"Wow, look at them." Gina stood on her tiptoes and waved at them. Leena saw them first and pulled the other two over.

"I didn't know you smoked, Pearl," Jules said.

"Oh, this?" Pearl held up the cigarette holder. It was

about a foot long and black with silver accents. "It's just an accessory for show."

"You girls look gorgeous, and everything is amazing!" Rose gushed. "Maddie, you've outdone yourself."

Maddie beamed. "Thanks. I did have a bit of help." Despite being thrilled about the outcome of the party, Maddie couldn't help but feel a little sad that Dex wasn't there to see it. He had done as much as she had to make it happen. Then her mind flashed to the look of triumph on Lorelei's face when she'd told Maddie that Dex was going to Portland with her instead, and she pushed thoughts of him away.

"Will you look at that?" Leena nodded toward the dance floor, where Henry and Aggie were whirling around. Aggie's skirt swirled out, and the red feather bobbed atop her head. As they watched, the couple ended the dance in a dramatic dip, and the crowed clapped.

"I didn't realize Henry had that in him," Rose said.

"Aggie must be special." Pearl winked.

"Lucky they didn't throw their backs out. He's not the only one with a surprise up his sleeve." Leena pointed toward the corner of the tent. "Look over there."

Maddie's jaw dropped. Constance Harbinger was standing at a high-top table in a gold lamé dress, chatting with Lorna and Belinda.

"Who knew that would ever happen?" Pearl asked.

"I did." Rose sounded confident. "Connie was always a nice person. She just had a bad thing happen to her, and it soured her for a bit. All it took was someone doing something nice for her."

"What did anyone do for her?" Leena asked.

"My Dex. He fixed up her house for her in his spare time," Rose leaned in and whispered. "But don't tell anyone. He doesn't like to let the word out that he does free work. She had really let the house go."

"It's really too bad he couldn't be here," Maddie said. A big reason they could have this party was because of Dex.

"Oh, didn't you hear?" Rose asked.

"Yeah, I know, he's in Portland looking for a place with Lorelei."

"No, dear. I'm afraid he isn't going to move in with Lorelei at all. Dex is staying in Shell Cove, and as far as I know, he should be here at this party."

This was good news, or was it? Why hadn't Dex mentioned it to her? Maybe they weren't as good of friends as she'd thought. Maybe he didn't think that his decision to stay in town would matter to her. Maybe the fact that they could become better friends… or something more… wasn't even anything that played into the decision.

"I wonder why Maddie looked sad when you mentioned that Dex was staying in town," Leena asked as they watched the three cousins drift off into the crowd.

"My guess is that he hasn't mentioned it to her and hearing it from me made her feel left out. That's a good sign. Means she cares," Rose said.

"He better get his butt here and let her hear it from him if he does care about her. But maybe he doesn't like her *that* way, though." Leena scanned the crowd. "I think I still have a chance to win that bet."

Rose laughed. "Maybe. I just want the two of them to be happy, whether or not they get together."

"How could anyone not be happy with this going on?" Pearl gestured at the crowd. "Not just this amazing party, but the whole town. This event is the thing that will change Shell Cove. I feel it in my bones."

"Me too. It's a change for the town. How will that change things for us?" Leena asked.

"More welcome wagon opportunities!" Rose rubbed her hands together.

Pearl nodded. "That's right. More people will move in."

"Before we get ahead of ourselves, maybe we should think about how we can help Chuck and Deena. You know, create opportunities so that the kids have a chance to see how they are right for each other," Leena suggested, even though she'd bet against them staying together. Rose suspected her sour attitude against couples and the way she was always betting against them was just a front. Leena was really an old softy at heart but didn't want anyone to see it.

"How about a town picnic? We need to celebrate," Pearl said.

"Yes! Everyone could bring signature dishes," Rose agreed.

Leena made a face. "I hope Maddie's is better than what she brought to the last town meeting."

Rose tucked a stray peacock feather into the side of her hat. "Let's hope."

"At least we know Gina will bring a fabulous pie," Pearl said. "She'd really excelled at that. She needs to do something with it, though. I showed her an empty shop downtown that would be perfect, but she seems a bit hesitant."

Leena cleared her throat and glanced around furtively.

Rose frowned. "What is it?"

Leena leaned toward them. "It's just that I happened to see a check from Gina on Ellison's desk the other day."

"Really?" Leena's daughter, Ellison, was a private investigator in town. She'd been a cop but had struck out on her own when she neared age fifty. "What would Gina need a PI for?"

"Beats me. I couldn't ask. You know how tight-lipped Ellie is about her clients."

"Very curious," Rose said. "Could she be looking into something about that empty shop?"

"Why would she need to investigate that?"

"No idea. Anyway, it's none of our business, and Dex is headed this way. I'd appreciate if we kept that little tidbit to ourselves." Leena made a zipping motion across her lips.

"Gram! You all look fantastic." Dex turned his charming smile on the ladies and kissed each of their hands, leaving them giggling.

"You're such a charmer." Pearl swatted him on the arm. "We're glad you're staying in town, but sorry about your girl."

Dex shrugged. He didn't look too sad about it, Rose noticed with satisfaction. "I think it was a long time coming. Shell Cove is my home and always will be."

"I'm glad to hear you say that." Rose kissed him on the cheek. "I selfishly am glad you won't be far."

"Me too." Dex scanned the crowd. "Have you seen Maddie?"

"She was just here. Maybe over by the bar? I think I see Jules over there."

"Okay, thanks. I need a drink anyway. Can I get you ladies anything?"

The three of them held up their full wineglasses. "We're all set."

"Okay, talk later." Dex headed toward the bar.

Rose jabbed Leena in the ribs. "See, looks like you better brace yourself for losing that bet."

CHAPTER THIRTY-ONE

*M*addie had danced, chatted, and even had a few glasses of champagne. It was great to celebrate with her cousins and the other towns-people she'd become friendly with, but something was missing.

She'd thought maybe Dex would show up, espe-cially after Rose's revelation. Maybe Dex wasn't the type who liked these sorts of parties. Funny, though, before he'd made plans with Lorelei, he'd seemed excited about the party. Maybe he was in a funk about their breakup, or maybe they'd already made up.

A few hours of partying had exhausted her, so she said her goodbyes and headed to Starfish Cottage. Once home, though, she couldn't sleep. Something was both-ering her.

After changing into a pair of comfortable jean

shorts and a T-shirt, she grabbed a couple of beers from the fridge, slipped out the back door barefoot, and started down the beach, heading for her special place down by the rocks.

The cool ocean water soothed her feet, which were aching from the high heels on the shoes she'd borrowed from Jules. The smells and sounds of the ocean and the stars twinkling in the dark sky lifted her spirits. This was her place, where she was meant to be, and now that the event was a success, she had hope that she'd be able to stay.

She sat down on the flat rock and imagined the future, when the town was thriving and the work on her cottage was finished. She had a clear picture now of how she wanted it to turn out. And now that Dex was staying in town, he would have the time to do what she wanted.

Thinking of Dex reminded her of the night they'd sat on these very rocks, and her good mood deflated. She'd thought that had been a special time, a pivotal time in their relationship where she'd discovered they had more in common than she'd first thought. She'd felt like they'd "had a moment." Was she the only one who had felt that way?

D<small>EX</small> <small>FELT</small> <small>SILLY</small> <small>IN</small> <small>HIS</small> 1930<small>S</small>-<small>STYLE</small> <small>SUIT</small> <small>NO</small> <small>MATTER</small> how much his grandmother gushed about how handsome he looked. The saving grace was that every other guy that had dressed for the party appeared to be just as uncomfortable.

The place looked great though, and there was a huge turnout. His heart swelled to see the town thriving once again.

"Hey, Dex. I wanted to thank you again for what you did for me." Constance Harbinger stood at his side. He barely recognized her all dressed up and smiling. Smiling wasn't something he'd seen her do often.

"You're very welcome. Thank you for digging into the town laws and making this all happen."

"Oh, I can't take much credit for that. It's mostly down to Maddie Montgomery. She's a real asset to the town."

"She sure is." Dex scanned the crowed over Constance's shoulder for Maddie. He wanted to congratulate her in person, and he also wanted to try to get back to the friendship that had been blossoming between them earlier. "Have you seen her?"

"Maddie? Oh, sure. She's here somewhere." Constance turned and looked out at the crowd. "Last I saw she was over by the railing in the corner there."

Dex saw a red feather above the crowd. Hadn't Nick mentioned something about her outfit having a headband with a big red feather? "Thanks. You enjoy the evening."

"You too!" Constance called after him as he made his way through the crowd.

There were so many people, he kept losing sight of the feather. Maddie sure was getting around. He turned the corner of the building where it had disappeared, practically running. No feather.

There it was, over on the other side of the tent!

Dex jostled his way through the boisterous crowd, trying not to elbow people out of his way.

"Oh, Dex! So glad to hear you are staying." Belinda Simms caught his arm. "Your grandmother is so happy."

Dex couldn't be rude to Belinda even though he wanted to pull away.

"I'm happy be near Gram. I guess maybe Lorelei wasn't really the one. Gram helped me see that." Dex's attention drifted to the crowd over Belinda's shoulder. Darn! The feather wasn't there anymore.

"That's nice. Looks like you need to get yourself a drink." Belinda gestured to his empty hands. "I'll just—"

"No need." Dex saw his way to exit gracefully. "I was on my way to the corner bar. Can I get you something?"

"No, I'm fine. You go." Belinda waved him off, and Dex breathed a sigh of relief. He'd taken a chance offering to get her a drink, but since she had a full one in her hand, it wasn't really much of a chance.

"Have a great time!" Dex spun in the direction he'd last seen the feather. Wait... was that it, bobbing above the crowd, heading toward the other side of the building? Why would Maddie be going over there? It was dark, and no one was there…. unless she wasn't alone.

Maybe he shouldn't interrupt her. That would be the smart thing. But even as he thought it, his feet were rushing toward the corner of the building.

He had almost caught up when she slipped around the side with a man in a black fedora. Tossing away all common sense, he rushed over after her.

"Hey, Maddie! I—"

She spun around, and Dex skidded to a stop.

It wasn't Maddie. It was Henry's new friend, Aggie, and it looked like he might have interrupted something between her and Henry.

"Dex! Hello! I'm flattered you mistook me for Maddie." Aggie laughed. "I'm a bit older."

"Oh, sorry. Nick mentioned that she was wearing a red dress with a big feather." He'd been chasing the wrong person all along!

"Oh, I see." Aggie touched the feather. "She was going to wear this, but it was too big and mine was too small, so we traded. She's in a lovely shade of hot pink now. But you won't find her here."

"I won't?"

"She went home."

"Oh." That was odd. Why would Maddie leave the party she'd worked so hard for?

"She seemed a little down in the dumps." Henry put his arm around Aggie's shoulders and leaned toward him, a sparkle in his eye. "She was asking about you though."

"She was?" Dex's heart lifted.

"Yep, seemed keen to see you. You can probably catch her since she just left a few minutes ago."

Dex didn't need to think about it. He said goodbye to Henry and Aggie and jogged for his truck. He had an idea of where Maddie might go if she was feeling down, and if they were going to get back on the path they'd been on before Lorelei screwed things up, it would be the perfect place for them to start.

CHAPTER THIRTY-TWO

*M*addie was about to open her second beer when movement caught her eye. She squinted down the beach, her heart jolting. Someone was coming!

She'd never considered that it might be dangerous to sit on this remote part of the beach alone. Shell Cove was such a safe place. She'd never heard of any crimes, much less a creepy stalker on the beach. Who would be out here at night, and why weren't they at the party?

She rose, her heart thudding. She could run, but the person was in between her and the cottage. The other direction was more remote; there wasn't a house or path off the beach for almost a quarter mile.

Wait. Something was familiar about the figure.

"Maddie?"

"Dex?"

Relief washed over her.

"I was looking for you at the party." He looked kind of silly but also kind of good in his pinstripe slacks and white shirt. She'd only ever seen him in his work clothes of jeans and a T-shirt.

"I got partied out. It was a busy day, and I needed some quiet time. So I came to my special place."

"Yeah, I can understand that. The party was a bit boisterous. I hope you don't mind me joining you."

"Not at all." Maddie sat back down and gestured toward one of the smooth rocks for him to sit on.

"Beer?" She held an unopened beer out to him.

"I don't want to drink your last one."

"Plenty more at the cottage. Take it." He took the beer, their hands brushing, eyes meeting. In that second, Maddie knew something had changed. He'd come looking for her, and even though she didn't want to read more into it, she felt a closeness, and it wasn't because he'd chosen to sit only a fraction of an inch away from her.

"The party was fantastic. Nice job." Dex tipped his beer toward her, and they clinked bottles.

"Thanks. I had a lot of help. Speaking of which, thanks for all of yours."

"Happy to do it." Dex sipped his beer and gazed up at the stars. "I want to apologize for acting weird."

"You weren't acting weird. You broke up with

someone that you'd been with for a long time. Of course that's going to be a little strange."

"Yeah, it is, but I think it was a long time coming. We weren't really happy together, but it happened so gradually it took me a while to figure that out. And I guess I kind of floated along. I didn't look at my long-term plan enough."

"Did you just say 'long term plan'?" Maddie looked at him sideways.

Dex laughed. "Yeah, well I guess you could say I didn't have one. But working with you must have rubbed off. You showed me that sometimes just going with the flow isn't a good idea."

"So you're coming around to my way of thinking," Maddie teased. She was flattered that he'd remembered some of her advice about planning.

"Don't get too smug about it. I still plan to fly by the seat of my pants most of the time."

Maddie laughed. "Well, since we're confessing, you taught me some things too."

His left brow quirked up. "Really?"

"Yep. And I do agree that sometimes having a rigid plan can be detrimental. If I hadn't relaxed my strict thinking about my plan, the event might not have come off as good as it did. I needed to be able to let go of the vision I'd planned to be able to see another way to set things up. So thanks for that."

"You're welcome."

The warmth in Dex's smile made her heart flip. "But don't you go getting too smug either. I'm still going to plan things like I usually do. I'll just be a little more open to changing."

"Well, then with your planning skills and my ability to pivot quickly, sounds like we might make a good team." Dex leaned in toward her, and Maddie felt herself drawn to meet him halfway.

"It sounds like we would." And then she leaned just another inch forward and kissed him.

CHAPTER THIRTY-THREE

Two weeks later....

"That should do it for the painting. What do you think?"

Maddie looked up from her task of arranging cheese and crackers on a plate. Dex stood in the living room, paintbrush in hand, admiring his handiwork on the wall which he'd just painted a cool light gray.

"Looks great." Maddie scanned the room. Over the past two weeks, they'd managed to finish ripping down old wallpaper, paint the walls, and install new flooring. The wall between the kitchen and living room was down, and the place looked gorgeous. Maddie still had to work on the cabinets, but she was pleased with the progress.

She still didn't have any furniture, but now that it

was painted and the flooring was in, she could have the store deliver the dark-gray sofa and light-blue accent pillows she and Dex had picked out together. Not that Dex was living there. It was way too early for that. But there had been a few dates, and even more important, they were friends and she trusted his opinion.

Nick's car pulled into the driveway. "Nick's here. Why don't you two grab the ice bucket and some beers and sit out on the deck while I finish this cheese tray? Gina and Jules should be here any minute."

"Sounds good." Dex washed the paintbrush in the sink and then filled the ice bucket. His lips brushed her cheek just as Nick knocked on the slider door.

Dex opened the door, and Nick poked his head in. "Hey, Maddie!"

"Hi, Nick. I'll be right out. You guys go ahead." Maddie turned back to the cheese with a smile. There was nothing she liked better than having her family and friends over, and since her duties with the event were finished, there had been a lot of time for that during the past two weeks.

She finished up the cheese and laid it in the middle of the tray. Then she spread some crackers on one side of the tray, added some grapes on the other, and grabbed a bottle of wine just as Jules and Gina arrived.

Gina had brought a peach pie, and she grabbed some dessert plates out of Maddie's cupboard. They all settled on the outdoor sectional shaded from the hot summer sun by a giant umbrella Jules and Gina had bought her as a housewarming gift. Since Starfish Cottage was off the beaten path and not near any public beaches, the long stretch of golden-white sand in front of them was empty except for a few sandpipers running along the edge of the surf. A slight sea breeze stirred the air.

"Here's to Shell Cove and good friends." Nick raised his beer, and they all leaned in to tap each other's drinks.

"Things have really picked up since the Marco Rosone event." Jules held up crossed fingers. "Let's hope it stays that way."

"It's all up to word of mouth now." Nick put his arm around Jules's shoulders. "We've had a few merchants coming in for loans now that business is picking up. That's a good sign."

"This pie is amazing." Dex had set aside his beer to focus on the pie. "You should open up a shop, Gina."

"Huh?" Gina looked up from her phone. Maddie had noticed that her cousin had been getting a lot of texts lately, and she'd been acting quite secretive about them.

"He said you should open a pie shop, like I've been telling you to do," Jules said.

"Oh, well, I don't know if I'm ready for that yet, but

thanks for your confidence." Gina glanced down at her phone again then turned it over so no one could see the screen.

"What's going on?" Maddie nodded toward the phone. "Secret admirer?"

Gina scoffed. "Hardly. Just the usual stuff. But enough about me. How about the town? I feel like things are looking up, and the motel is booked out for almost the entire summer."

"Really?" Dex looked up from his pie. "That's great."

Maddie felt a pang of guilt. Earlier in the month, she'd been focused on the event and then on her cottage. She hadn't helped out at the motel at all. "I'm going to start putting in regular hours there again."

"Don't worry about it." Jules waved her off. "We have it handled. I might put you on laundry duty though."

Maddie laughed. "Maybe we'll have enough money to hire someone for that soon."

"With all the rooms booked, it won't be long." Gina settled back and sipped her wine. "Though I am upset our long-term resident won't be staying much longer."

Maddie leaned forward to grab a cracker then stick a slice of cheddar on top. "Aggie? Oh no! I thought she might be staying indefinitely. Poor Henry!"

"Actually, she is staying, just not at the motel," Nick

said. "She's getting a permanent place in town. I guess Gramps is really hard to resist."

Jules smiled at him. "Runs in the family."

Gina made a gagging noise. "We don't need to go down that road. But speaking of relationships, there might be some drama at the motel."

"Why do you say that?" Maddie asked.

"Chuck's son, Cole, and Deena's daughter, Sam, both made reservations at the motel for the same week."

"I remember Chuck and Deena wanted them to come. We gave them a discount. But why is that a problem?" Maddie asked.

"Since they don't approve of Chuck and Deena's relationship, they might be at odds. Sam thinks Chuck is taking advantage of Deena, and Cole thinks Deena is taking advantage of Chuck." Gina flipped her phone over and glanced at the screen quickly before flipping it back.

"I could see how that can be problematic," Jules said. "But it won't take them long to see that Chuck and Deena are very nice and that they are made for each other."

"Maybe," Gina said. "But you know how people are. Once they are invested in an idea, they don't want to let go of it."

"True." Maddie knew that better than anyone. "Hopefully they will come to their senses."

"I hope so for Chuck and Deena's sake," Maddie said.

"I don't know. I think we may be in for an interesting summer," Gina said.

"Nothing wrong with that." Maddie settled back into the cushions, and they lapsed into the easy conversation of good friends. She was optimistic about the rest of the summer. The town was starting to thrive, the motel was booked, and she had a summer full of beach nights and get-togethers on her deck. What more could she ask for?

****

I HOPE YOU ENJOYED YOUR VISIT TO SHELL COVE. IF you like Hallmark style small town sweet romances, they you're going to love my brand new and very first Christmas Romance - Christmas at Cozy Holly Inn!

Join my newsletter for sneak peeks of my latest books and release day notifications:

https://lobsterbay1.gr8.com

Another Wish (Book 2)

Meredith Summers writes cozy mysteries as USA Today Bestselling author Leighann Dobbs and crime fiction as L. A. Dobbs.

She spent her childhood summers in Ogunquit Maine and never forgot the soft soothing feeling of the beach. She hopes to share that feeling with you through her books which are all light, feel-good reads.

Join her newsletter for sneak peeks of the latest books and release day notifications:

https://lobsterbay1.gr8.com

This is a work of fiction.

None of it is real. All names, places, and events are products of the author's imagination. Any resemblance to real names, places, or events are purely coincidental, and should not be construed as being real.

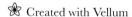